Treaty Brides

THE SECRET BRIDE

SAMANTHA CAYTO

The Secret Bride
ISBN # 978-1-80250-530-6

Interior text design by Claire Siemaszkiewicz
Pride Publishing

Published in 2023 by Pride Publishing, United Kingdom.

Pride Publishing is an imprint of Totally Entwined Group Limited.

Pride Publishing books by Samantha Cayto

Single Books
One Night in a Dungeon
Man Candy
Against a Rising Tide

Alien Slave Masters
The Captain's Pet
The Rebellious Pet
The Untamed Pet
The Captive Pet
The Inconvenient Pet
The Undercover Pet

Alien Blood Wars
Blood Dance
Dangerous Dance
Slave Dance
Star Dance
Mating Dance
Healing Dance
Smoke Dance
Final Dance: Part One
Final Dance: Part Two

Treaty Brides
Boi Bride
The Diplomat's Bride
Stolen Bride
The Substitute Bride
The Secret Bride

Anthologies
His Rules: Safeword
Right Here, Right Now: Never the Groom

Collections

Rules of Summer: In the Heat of the Dungeon
Dark and Deadly: Dream Demon
S.W.A.L.K.: His True Heart
His Harem: Room for Elijah

THE SECRET BRIDE

Chapter One

Lord Cariad of Kenworth kept his focus on the paper in front of him and ignored the busyness of the sailors around him. With the lateness of the day, the beating hot sun wasn't as much of a danger to his fair skin, and he prized any time he could take on deck. Spending most of the voyage below in the small cabin he shared with two junior officers was depressing, and the confined space was stifling. At least up here there was a cool breeze, even if it was also populated with large men who made him uncomfortable. Not that any of them dared look sideways at him… They all believed he warmed the captain's bed, which was a ridiculous assumption, given that he was only ever in the man's cabin alone with him to go over his latest maps. He supposed men didn't need much time to fuck, although why anyone would seek an activity that made one even more sticky and sweaty was beyond him.

As he hunched over the images he etched on his paper, a shadow fell over them. He stiffened only a moment, then forced himself to relax again. "Good afternoon, Captain." He only glanced up at the man before returning his gaze to his drawing.

"What is this you do?" There was censure in the tone.

Cariad chose to ignore the disapproval. "It's important to memorialize what we find." He did look up now at the captain's stern face. "When people wonder what the fight with the Swarm was all about, drawings such as these will speak more loudly of the horror than mere words."

He gazed at his drawing again, his stomach tightening at the images he drew of the death and destruction the Swarm had wrought on the small island village they'd come across the day before. Everything had been decimated, with buildings burned and bodies of mostly fighting-aged men littering the ground. The rest of the inhabitants had vanished, no doubt carried off by the Swarm to become slaves or sacrifices. Even the livestock had been slaughtered and butchered. The sight of so much savagery had haunted his thoughts and dreams all night. He had to do something to help, and this was all he could think of.

The captain grunted. "I should never have let you join my men in their exploration. It was obvious from the wrecked ships that the Swarm had been there. You have too delicate of a nature to see such things."

"I appreciate your concern, sir, but I am stronger than I look." Opening the top of his lap desk, he stuck the drawing in with the rest of his sketches and closed it again, hoping it would put an end to the discussion.

The captain chuckled. "I imagine you are…with the right incentive. But soft, as well, yes? Where it counts," he added, the lecherous implication clear.

Cariad swallowed back a retort. He walked a fine line on this ship, keeping the man in charge at arm's length while not doing anything that could lead to punishment for insolence. Not that he worried overly much about his own safety… As a nobleman and cousin to the king, he was protected from any overt violence, but his work mattered. If the captain confined him to his quarters, mapping out these waters accurately would become impossible. He needed to see everything around him with a clear view to draw accurate maps.

As he'd found it useful to deflect, he asked a question that kept swirling inside his head. "Sir, how do you suppose the Swarm managed to sink so many boats?" The small island harbor had been littered with broken pieces of wood, submerged sterns and sails torn to shreds.

"I don't know." The man's tone indicated that Cariad had been successful. He was now thinking of his duty and not his loins. "I've never seen the like, and I have waged battles on the sea many times. It's disturbing. If I don't know what the danger is, I can't protect my ship and men."

A letch he may be, but the captain was good at his duty, keeping a tightly run ship with a fair yet firm hand. He hadn't been indifferent to the death and destruction his men had reported back to him. And he did seem to appreciate the work Cariad did, praising his skill, even if he did so with a leer more often than not.

Sensing that it was a good time to take his leave, Cariad stood. "I should get washed for supper."

Ambrose's gaze slid down his body. "An excellent idea, my lord. You have sweated through your shirt."

Cariad resisted the urge to hunch his shoulders to hide the spots that stuck to the skin of his chest. He didn't understand why the sight of his skinny frame would be enticing to anyone. As far as he was concerned, he didn't have the body to interest men…or women, for that matter. He resented the fact that he was supposed to want such attention at all. "Yes, sir. I'll see you at your table later."

"Excellent. And afterward I want you to stay with me to go over some of your most recent maps."

"As you wish, Captain." As a dance, this was getting tedious. Most every night, the man made up some reason for Cariad to stay later with him. It led to pressure on him to drink and get chummy, with the obvious goal of getting him into bed. The entire effort was tiresome, but there was no way to avoid it without causing significant resentment.

He'd taken only one step toward the hatchway when the lookout's cry sounded from his perch high up on the mast. "Ship ahoy!" Then he said something that caused Cariad's blood to freeze. "The Swarm."

There was a moment when everyone around him froze from the news. The captain was the first to leap into action. "Battle stations!" Grabbing Cariad by the shoulder, he gave him a shove. "Go to my cabin. Sean is there setting my table. Keep him with you. Bolt the door shut and don't come out, no matter what. *Now*!" he added when Cariad didn't move fast enough.

With his heart in his throat, Cariad scrambled to obey, even as his mind reeled at the sudden turn of events. He'd been out in these waters for a long time and never had they spotted a Swarm ship. They were a scouting clipper, meant to be fast and nimble. And while the crew were trained to fight, he thought they would have trouble holding their own against the vicious warriors of the Swarm. Their best hope was to outrun them. But as soon as he had that idea, there was another cry from the lookout. Cariad scanned the other side of the boat before he scrambled down the staircase and nearly stumbled at the sight of a second Swarm ship heading their way.

We can't fight them both.

He had to swallow his panic as he made his way to the captain's cabin and practically threw himself through the door. Tossing his portable desk onto the floor, he turned to throw the two bolts that would only slow down any attackers. Then he stood panting as if he'd run a long distance and strained to hear what was happening up on deck.

"What's going on?" Ambrose's cabin boy, Sean, came through the archway leading to the captain's mess. His eyes were wide with fright.

Although Cariad was only a few years older than the boy, he felt responsible, not that there was anything he could do to protect him. "The Swarm have found us. There are two ships," he added, swallowing hard and looking away from the sheer terror on Sean's face now.

"We can't fight two!" the boy wailed.

"I know."

"What do we do?"

"Stay here. It's the safest place for us. And we do what we can to protect our people."

Sean wrung his hands. "How?"

"By keeping our secrets." So saying, Cariad hurried over to the captain's desk and started pulling out his own maps and the man's logs.

"Hey, you can't touch those." Sean came and reached out to stop him.

"We have to get rid of all this before the Swarm gets their hands on it. They can't know how much we've learned. It will take away any element of surprise our fleet and the Chainers might have."

Sean's expression grew stern. "That's not for us to decide. You're only the cartographer, even if you are a lord. The captain will tan my hide if I let you destroy any of this."

Cariad was certain that the captain would have no chance to mete out any punishment. If he weren't killed outright, the man would be taken prisoner. They all would. Then they'd learn firsthand the fate of the people from the village, and all the rumors concerning the Swarm would either be confirmed or dispelled. Getting the answers wouldn't bring them any comfort. Of that, he was sure.

He opened his mouth to explain the obvious to Sean. A loud sound, followed by a rocking motion that made it hard to keep their feet under them, cut his words off. As one, he and Sean raced to the large window on the starboard side of the cabin. One of the Swarm ships had closed in on them. Smoke curled out from open ports on the side of the vessel. As Cariad squinted to see what was there, another loud sound boomed. He jumped back and collided with Sean at the sight of a large iron ball flying toward them. They both lost their footing and tumbled to the floor when their ship shuddered from what had to be an impact.

Sean clutched at his arm. "What was that? How did they make that thing fly? I didn't see a catapult."

Cariad's mind whirled to find an answer. It came to him quickly, and once more he froze with dread. "They've weaponized fireworks."

"What?" Sean cringed against him as another explosive sound whined through the window.

Cariad held the boy in his arms for a moment to give them both comfort, little as it was. "They've found a way to create the same kind of explosion needed for fireworks and have upped the power to throw what appears to be an iron ball at us. That explains the destruction in the village harbor. They don't need the room necessary for a catapult. The balls fire straight at their target."

There was more violent rocking of the ship, and the screams of the crew as they fought to control it and save themselves were terrible. Cariad wanted to stop-up his ears, but he didn't have the luxury of giving into his terror. The outcome of the fight was obvious to him now more than ever. He had to protect his people's secrets, even as he understood that his life, one way or another, was going to be forfeit.

"Come on." He pushed Sean away, then helped him to his feet. "We need to get rid of these papers." He scrambled back to the captain's desk, struggling to stay upright as the ship trembled and swayed with each new onslaught.

"No. We can't give up hope of being victorious."

Clutching maps to his chest, Cariad rounded on the boy. "Don't be an idiot! We have already lost this battle. Soon the Swarm will board us from both sides and take anything of value before scuttling the Intrepid."

The cabin boy's lower lip wobbled, and tears pooled in his eyes. But he made no more objection, merely grabbed the captain's heavy logbook. "How do we destroy them?"

Cariad gnawed on his upper lip. Burning would be best, but there was no way to get to the galley's fire.

Simply tearing the paper up wouldn't do the trick, because there wasn't time to do a proper job of it. The solution came to him then. "The privy." The captain had the luxury of having use of a hole that went straight into the sea instead of a smelly trough. It was the only course of action.

He hurried through the mess and into the privy, Sean at his heels. More explosions sent them careening into walls, but they managed to stay upright. Cariad lifted the cover and stared into the dark churning sea far below. With only a moment's hesitation, he tossed the maps he'd labored over down into the water. Then he helped Sean toss the logbook after them. They made three more trips until the captain's papers and all the maps were consigned to the ocean. There was nothing left to do except wait for their fates to play out.

The ship listed to one side, sending them onto the floor and sliding against the far wall. Through the window, they got their first look at the men of the Swarm, as they were finally boarded. Cariad closed his eyes, terrified of the nightmarish view of enormous creatures with deathly pale skin and ink-black hair. If these weren't demons, he couldn't imagine who would be.

He and Sean remained huddled together, taking as much courage as they could from each other. The sounds of a pitched battle reached their ears easily enough. It was impossible to block it out, yet worse by far was the sudden silence that told them the fighting was over. There was no doubt as to who the victors were, but it still startled him and nearly made him weep when the door shuddered from the efforts to break it open.

"Come on." Cariad staggered to his feet and helped Sean do the same. "We mustn't give them the satisfaction of seeing how scared we are."

Bold words were followed by a dry mouth and pounding heart as the wood of the door splintered from an ax. When there was a sufficiently big hole, a bloody hand was shoved through to throw the bolts. Then that same hand opened the door to let in the biggest man Cariad had ever seen. As he took in the sight of the enemy—from the long, black hair braided with beads to the stern pale face with high, slashing cheekbones and eyes that looked like they glowed—he couldn't help but wonder why the gods had designed these demons with such arresting beauty. He blinked rapidly, as if he could clear what had to be a mirage. Surely the beings he feared the most couldn't cause his heart to stutter for an entirely different reason. Yet as the man approached, he had to struggle to remind himself that this was pure evil advancing on him, someone destined to make the rest of his life a miserable and probably short one.

The Swarm warrior stopped a short distance away and cocked his head as his eyes—now visibly violet in color—bore into Cariad. "Well, well, what do we have here?"

Balthazar studied the pale-haired boy standing in front of him, trying to appear brave, yet whose fear was a palpable thing. This was an intriguing development—one he couldn't keep his gaze off of. It wasn't merely his beauty, although that was stunning. More, it was the fact that he was dressed as a civilian. His companion was pretty, too, but his uniform proclaimed him a cabin boy and therefore of no real interest. Who was this well-dressed young man? Surely the Moorcondians were not so foolish as to invite the curious to join them on their scouting missions.

He took another step closer and couldn't help smiling when the boys started to take a step back, only to be brought up short by the wall behind them. "There is nowhere for you to go. Who are you?" he added, focusing his gaze on the blond-haired boy. He could practically see the thoughts turning behind those interesting eyes. They were green and gold, unlike anything he'd seen before. *Quite alluring.* "It's not a difficult question," he added when an answer was not forthcoming.

With a visible swallow, the boy finally replied. "I'm Cariad."

Balto chuckled. "Such a clever boy, Cariad, to know your own name. Now answer my actual question—and perhaps I need to be clearer. What are you doing on this ship? And don't say you're a cabin boy. That's what he is," he added, pointing at the quivering companion.

The one called Cariad lifted his chin in the next instant, an impressive show of courage. "It depends on your definition of what a cabin boy is. I am the captain's…doxy."

"Ah." Now here was a truly inventive answer and one that caused his cock, already hard from the battle, to jerk. It only served to pique his interest, however. Bed-warmers could be very pretty for sure, yet he doubted one would have the look of someone raised in good health and dressed in fine, if plain, clothing. His voice held tones of culture, as well, compared to the rough voices of other Moorcondians he'd just encountered. This mystery made him want the boy even more and for reasons that had nothing to do with his straining cock. He could prove to be immensely useful.

He beckoned to them. "Come." When neither boy moved, he added, "You may walk to the deck on your own feet, or I and my men can sling you over our shoulders and carry you up. Your choice."

With a glare, the boy said, "That will not be necessary." He squared his shoulders and, clasping the other boy's arm, moved toward the door.

Balto was almost disappointed that he wouldn't have a chance to get his hands on the enticing body. *Later.* He glared at his men in a silent command to not touch as he started to follow his captive. Something under the captain's desk caught his eye. "Stop!"

He reached down and dragged out a portable writing desk, the kind one balanced on their lap. Curious, he opened it up and had to catch the gasp of surprise before it jumped out of his mouth. The top drawings showed the destruction of their most recent pillage. A quick look through the rest of the papers showed that there were more, each one drawn with impressive detail. Here was an answer to his questions about the boy, he was sure of it.

He looked at Cariad, who stood by the door staring at him with concern. "Did you do these?"

The boy shrugged in studied indifference. "I get bored. There's nothing for me to do when the captain is otherwise occupied with his duties."

"You had to have seen this to draw it so accurately. I'm surprised the captain would allow his pretty piece of ass to wander so far away from him."

The boy's pale cheeks pinked up. "I have a vivid imagination, that's all."

"Ah. I suppose that's a good quality in a whore." When the boy dropped his gaze, he let the matter go. "Up with you, then."

He followed them to the deck, the writing desk under his arm. During his brief time below, the Moorcondians who'd survived the fight had been herded to one side to cross over onto his brother's ship—all except the captain... He knelt in front of his new master, his brother Malachi. The man's gaze tracked the arrival of the two boys. Sadness crossed his face and something more, as he homed in on Cariad in particular. The ship listed suddenly, testament to how much water it was taking in. It would sink quickly. Balto grabbed hold of Cariad before he tumbled backward. A shudder ran through the boy's body before he wrenched himself free. Balto let him go. There would be time enough to impose his will.

He forced himself to smile as he spoke with his brother. "Look what treasure I've found, Mal."

Malachi's attention switched from gloating over the captain to the two boys. "You always have the best of luck in that regard, Balto." He took a few steps closer. "Fresh meat is always welcome on a long voyage."

Because his brother's gaze had fixed on Cariad, Balto had to stake his claim. He grabbed the boy by the hair, anchoring him in place and ignoring the brief struggle to get free of his hold. "Indeed, and I must claim this one as my prize."

Mal sneered briefly, but they'd already agreed that he would have the honor of bringing back their captives and offering the Moorcondian captain to their mother as a sacrifice. He was petty enough to want it all, yet sufficiently smart not to wage an open dispute with him. Mal was the elder of them, but Balto commanded great respect and loyalty from the men around them. "Of course. This one looks to be younger, and I bet untried." He pulled the cabin boy into his embrace by grabbing his ass. "I do love breaking them in."

"No!" The obviously terrified boy struggled to get free.

Mal put a stop to that by grasping his hair and slapping him hard. "Hold your tongue. I don't need to let you keep it to take pleasure from you." He leered into the now-crying boy's face. "You'll have to think of a way to convince me of its usefulness."

Cariad tried to lunge forward, his mouth open. Balto tugged him back and clasped a hand over those luscious lips. "Don't be stupid. You can't help him, but if you are clever, you will do as you're told and maybe you can be of use to your people after all." He kept his voice low, the words for the blond boy's ears only.

With another shudder, Cariad went still. Small tremors conveyed how hard it was for him to stay under control. He was smart, of that Balto was sure. And perhaps the boy would prove to be a gift dropped into Balto's lap, the key to solving the problem of how to put his plan into motion. It didn't do to get one's hopes up. He'd learned that harsh lesson as a boy in his own home. His long days as a marauder for his people had only reinforced that knowledge, to his bitter disappointment. The desk he clutched under his arm held the proof to how impotent he'd been so far. Maybe, by pure chance, the tide had finally turned in his favor.

Balto pushed the boy toward the railing as the ship once more warned of its impending sinking. "I am away to my ship, brother. I have all that I want from here, and I wish you a speedy return home."

"You as well, Balto, and good hunting in the meantime. When we meet again at the citadel, I expect you to have more prizes. You know how much our illustrious mother demands her tribute. Don't disappoint her as you've been doing lately. We wouldn't want her to worry that you can't be trusted to pull your weight without me to urge you to it."

Balto bared his teeth in their way of smiling at each other, cheerfulness with a hint of menace. "Worry not, Mal. I'm setting course farther into Chain waters. Where there's one Moorcondian ship, there may be others. I look forward to engaging with a new enemy." He pushed Cariad to the planks bridging the sinking ship with his own. "Climb over and don't even think about dropping into the sea. I'd only have to go in after you, and that would make me very angry."

Cariad scowled at him. "As if I would give you the satisfaction, you monster. My people will destroy you!"

Admiring the guts of the boy, he smiled in response. "They are welcome to try. In the meantime, you're mine."

Chapter Two

Cariad tried not to let his terror show as he was forced below the deck of the Swarm ship, the firm grip of its captain ensuring that he didn't break free. Not that he wanted to, in any event... Already they were casting off to leave the area, while the Intrepid groaned in her death throes. He didn't dare look back, as the sight of his most recent home being consigned to the sea would only serve to reinforce his predicament. He was a prisoner of the Swarm and his fate sealed with his lie of who and what he was. Whatever his captor had intended to do with him in theory before he'd blurted out the only thing that had come to mind, for certain he would avail himself of a Moorcondian whore's talents now. Although Cariad himself had little interest in bed sport, he understood that he was an outlier among men. Most of them spent their entire lives looking to stick their dick into something. The naked hunger in the Swarm captain's eyes confirmed that he was no different.

Cariad couldn't stop the shudder that racked him as he contemplated what was about to happen and might have tripped if not for the fingers clamped around his arm like a vise, keeping him up upright and moving. The truth be told, he had no interest in remaining above deck, either. As the captain tugged him along, the crew eyed him with varying degrees of interest. Each one of them was bigger than the other, including a fair number of females. The Moorcondian fleet had only a smattering of women in its ranks, mostly logistical officers. From what he'd seen, the Chainers had only a few more than that. This was different. Nearly half the people he glimpsed as he stumbled beside the captain had curves as well as height and muscle. All he could think was that if this crew was representative of the Swarm, his people had little chance to be victorious against them. *No wonder they decimate all they encounter.*

Besides the crew, there wasn't that much different about this ship from any other he'd been on. There was comfort in that, at least. His imagination had run wild with expectations of skull decorations and screams of the tortured. But there was none of that. Except for a spicy scent that permeated everything, the ship held nothing frightening—other than the crew and its captain, of course. The man who'd claimed him strode down the stairs and hallway with purposeful steps. It wasn't hard to imagine where they were headed, so there was no surprise when the man flung open a stout door and pulled Cariad into a large cabin.

As with the rest of the ship, the room was typical of what one might expect of the captain's personal space. Here again, there was the usual—a bed, desk, table and chairs, trunks tucked away and an alcove that probably led to the privy. Everything was dark wood and silk trappings, clean and smelling strongly of that spice. Cariad would have almost relaxed at the normalcy of it all, except there was a loud screech the moment they entered the cabin, the sound making him jump. He looked for the source of the noise and found a monkey squatted inside a cage hanging from the ceiling. Not that the confinement functioned as one would expect, the door to it being wide open. Cariad shrunk against his captor in instinctive revulsion. There was something unnerving about the almost-human faces of these strange creatures, and the manner in which they scurried around gave him the feeling he was under constant threat of attack.

The captain merely chuckled. "Now, now, Pia, be nice. This is my new guest, and you must get used to sharing the space with him." The man looked at Cariad. "There is no need to be frightened of her. She won't hurt you…unless you try to do me harm."

Pulling away, Cariad tried to show indifference. "It doesn't bother me if you keep a disgusting pet, so long as it stays in its cage."

The captain arched one eyebrow. "*She*. And someone who lets any man willing to pay stick his dick into him is hardly in a position to judge her harshly. She is very tidy and grooms herself meticulously. She's also a good companion to those who treat her well." He went to his desk and, pulling open the long top drawer, stuck Cariad's writing desk inside.

Cariad tried to hide his worry that his drawings somehow brought too much attention on him and shrugged. "I won't bother her if she doesn't bother me."

That earned him another chuckle before the Swarm captain pulled him to the far end of the cabin and all but tossed him onto the bed. His heart raced and his breath caught in his throat as he clutched at the bedding. He tried to look nonchalant, as any whore would under the circumstances. He feared, however, that he had the wide-eyed stare of a lamped rabbit in a field at night. And, gods, but the monkey would be watching everything that transpired in the room, adding a bizarre creepy factor into the rest of his living nightmare.

The Swarm captain loomed over the bed, his gaze boring a hole into him, as if reading his thoughts. With his layered clothing of leather pants and tunic, it was impossible to tell if the man was aroused, and his eyes gave nothing away about what churned inside his head. Not that it mattered… Of course, he intended to take his pleasure with Cariad. The only question was how and whether Cariad had any chance of keeping up the pretense of being a bed-warmer by profession. Having zero experience with sex of any kind, the obvious answer was no, none whatsoever. Then what? He'd have to make up another lie to explain who he was and why he'd been on the Intrepid.

He had to plumb the depths of his limited imagination—and fast. That would take some doing, given that he'd never played fantasy games as a child, preferring to study the real world around him. If there were a worse person to spin a yarn or keep up a pretense, he was unaware of them. There was no help for it, though. The truth would put his people in more jeopardy. The Swarm captain would try to force information out of him, and he wasn't certain he could resist the persuasiveness of whatever horrible torture the Swarm could devise. His bravery had never been put to the test in such a way, and he held no illusion that he was strong enough to keep his mouth shut.

Time dragged on to a nerve-scraping degree before the man finally spoke. "Stay there...and touch nothing." He glanced at the monkey. "Watch over him, Pia."

With that, he was gone, leaving Cariad alone in the cabin—except for the monkey, who stared at him with a disturbing intelligence in her eyes—and shaking with both relief and fear. Now that he was alone, he could let his feelings show. No matter what words that terrible creature understood, she wasn't capable of tattling on him. *Is she?* It was a ridiculous fear that he forced out of his mind. Wrapping his arms around his knees, he let the shuddering come and rocked to bring himself some comfort. But when the first tear trickled down his cheek, he swiped at it angrily and forced himself to get under control. He would not give his captor the satisfaction of him having red eyes and puffy cheeks. Bullies loved seeing the effect they had on their victims. His older brother had taught him the best way to deal with it was to pretend their efforts had failed. It wasn't clear whether the theory held when one was dealing with a monster instead of village boys, however. He was resolved, regardless, not to beg or plead when the man took what he wanted from him. Being Lord Cariad of Kenworth meant something. His family honor dictated he be strong and take whatever came his way with as much courage as he could muster.

Accepting the captain's orders as a sensible thing to acquiesce to, he stayed sitting on the bed, taking in his surroundings and resisting the urge to snoop about. He feared such activity would cause the monkey to screech at him, in any event. If he was very good and lucky, he might have the time and opportunity later to explore what useful information the man kept in his private space. The cage the monkey squatted in was free of bodily waste. Surely she left to do her business at some point. And Cariad also had to operate on the assumption that he'd eventually be freed. Not giving away any knowledge of his people and the Chainers was only half of his duty. The other was to glean whatever he could that would give them an advantage over the Swarm. Really, if he thought about it with a clear head, this was an excellent opportunity. He would make the most of his situation instead of dwelling on how awful it was. It might even be true that he was the first person to be in a position to do more than survive being captured by the Swarm.

His new thoughts buoyed his mood and he lay on the bed, staring up at the plain wooden ceiling, trying to rest for the ordeal that was soon to come. He only jumped a little bit when the door opened again sometime later. It wasn't the captain who entered, however. A girl, a little younger than he was, came in with a wicker basket tucked under her arm. Her steps were almost lighthearted, and she shot him a grin as she shut the door behind her, then stood staring at him. Cariad looked at her with equal frankness, not having seen anyone like her before. She wasn't as big as the other members of the crew, and her appearance was far different. Instead of having bone-white skin, hers was more like the color of tea. She was darker than the Chainers, and her hair, which hung in dozens of beaded braids, appeared to be more textured, almost curly. Her clothing was simple, as well—a dark red tunic over black cloth trousers. The only leather was in her belt and boots. And she carried no weapons that he could see.

The girl looked away and headed toward the cage. "Good evening to you, Pia. I have your dinner." The monkey made a chittering sound before leaping out of her cage and landing on the girl's shoulder. Instead of screaming like a sensible person, she merely laughed. "Yes, yes, I know you're hungry." Reaching into her basket, she pulled out a piece of fruit and put it into the tiny hands that, like the face, appeared very human. "That should hold you while I see to the captain's guest."

The girl approached the bed and stared at Cariad with a disturbing, yet not menacing, intensity. The monkey ignored him while she nibbled on her food. "Everyone said you were different. I've never seen hair that color before, and you're not very big."

"Neither are you." Cariad couldn't keep the retort to himself.

The girl simply laughed as she stopped by the side. "You're right." Sitting on the edge of the bed, she set the basket between them. "I've brought you supper."

Her words and the scents wafting toward him reminded Cariad that he hadn't eaten in a long while. Through the cabin's long window, he could see that night had fallen. His stomach even rumbled. He put his palm against it, but he couldn't let his hunger cause him to let down his guard. "Why?"

The girl cocked her head. "Why what?"

"Why are you bringing me food?" Such kindness didn't fit in with everything he'd heard about the Swarm. It was suspicious, although he couldn't imagine the Swarm had any reason to poison or sedate him. If they wanted him dead, a knife would get the job done—or they could simply throw him overboard. And if the captain wanted to force himself on him? Well, the man had the advantage of strength, not to mention that he'd already effectively offered to provide the sex. That's what whores did, after all. There was no need to make him compliant by drugging him.

"Captain Balthazar told me to, and I always obey him." She tapped a small marking on her cheek next to her earlobe. "I belong to him."

Cariad's stomach clenched as the import of her words and the mark became clear. "You're a slave."

"Yes." She nodded and grinned as if he'd made a pleasant comment on the weather.

He dropped his gaze. "I'm sorry."

"For what?" The girl blinked at him, obviously perplexed.

"That you've been enslaved," he explained, trying to be clear and figuring the poor thing didn't really understand her predicament or had been forced to stop questioning or resenting what had become of her life.

She shrugged as she opened her basket. "I was born a slave. And Captain Balthazar is the best of masters. He's letting me apprentice to the ship's cook. Someday I'll be the one running the galley."

Far from easing his worry, her words made him sadder. Her easy acceptance of her lot was born from knowing nothing else. Likely she considered having a chance to perform a job she enjoyed and perhaps not being beaten or raped every day constituted a good life. Or maybe part of her role on the ship was to keep the crew happy, too. Just because there was no visible sign of violence on her body didn't mean there wasn't any. He expected he'd come across others living with the Swarm who felt the same way. *Not me. Never me.* He knew what it was like to live freely and intended to do everything in his power to have that life again. In the meantime, he needed to keep up his strength and the pot of something the girl lifted from her basket did smell amazing.

She held it out to him with a spoon. "Stew."

Cariad took them from her and peered into the thick, gold liquid. "What's in it?"

"Are you so used to having your pick of food that you can choose what to eat?" Before he could answer, she giggled. "Fish, salt pork, beans and root vegetables. Cook let me make it myself. And yes, here's more fruit, Pia," she added when the monkey's now-empty paw snaked its way past her shoulder and toward the basket. The creature took the offering and settled back on her perch. The slave girl acted as if it were perfectly natural for a monkey to sit there—and likely it was.

Feeling a bit like a spoiled brat, Cariad dipped his spoon in the stew and took a tentative taste. It was delicious, flavorful with spices he didn't recognize, thick and warming as it slid down his throat. He had no trouble eating a bigger mouthful, not really caring if it was doctored with something he wouldn't like. The grin on the girl's face told him that he pleased her with his enthusiasm. Reaching inside the basket once more, she pulled out a small loaf of bread and pulled off a chunk for him. He accepted it readily and dipped it into his stew. It was surprisingly fresh and equally delicious.

The slave girl said nothing more for a while as he scarfed down his meal. Then, "What's your name?"

He hesitated only a moment, thinking he should probably provide a false one. It seemed pointless, however, as there was no reason to believe the Swarm would glean anything useful from the information. And he'd already blurted it out to his captor anyway, he remembered, in that initial moment of panic. "Cariad."

"How pretty. I'm Tashasrinivasalina. Tasha," she added when he gazed at her over the rim of his spoon.

"I'm pleased to make your acquaintance, Tasha," he said before taking another mouthful of stew.

"You speak as pretty as you look. Here, you must be thirsty." So saying, she got up from the bed and went to a shelf with a high edge built into the wall. The monkey took the opportunity to scamper off her shoulder, onto the nearby desk and from there, leap into her cage. Tasha paid the creature no mind. She took a flask from the shelf and brought it over. "Some cider. The captain won't mind."

Putting the almost-empty bowl on the mattress, he took the offered drink, unstopped it and smelled its contents. It was sweet and with no noticeable fermentation, so he drank a little, then a lot. He hadn't realized he was so parched. Before he knew it, the flask was mostly empty. "Oh." He handed it back. "Sorry. I hope you won't get into trouble for this."

Tasha shrugged. "I'll refill it tomorrow. Tending to the captain's needs is part of my duties."

Cariad's stomach clenched once more as he considered the import of her words. If nothing else, he could hope that his presence would spare her the almost certainly odious job of warming the captain's bed. "You'll get a rest from that with me here. He has me now to take care of his *needs*." Cariad forced himself to finish his meal. Who knew when he might get to eat again?

"You clean and do laundry?" Her question was asked with such an innocent earnestness that he couldn't believe she was teasing him.

Clearing his throat, he said, "I can if I have to, but I was referring to…." He looked pointedly down at the bed.

Tash didn't respond right away. When she did, it was with a laugh. "Oh no. I don't do *that*. My father would be very cross if I did," she added with another grin.

Cariad scraped the bottom of his bowl. "Do your father's feelings matter to the captain?" Undoubtedly the man was also a slave, a comfort to her to have family, yet her father must mourn his daughter's lot every day.

Her answer surprised him. "Of course they do." With no further explanation, the girl gathered up the remnants of his meal and packed up the basket. Then she returned the flask to its shelf before going to rub her fingers down the monkey's back while making cooing noises, as if the creature were a baby. She turned away. "I must go now. Cleaning up the galley is also my duty, and it has been a long day." She went to the door.

"Thank you. I appreciate the wonderful meal."

"I'm glad you liked it. Who knows what you Moorcondians like to eat?" She shrugged and left.

Alone again with the monkey and his thoughts, Cariad started to worry himself over what was to come when the captain returned. There was nothing to be gained by fretting. He could imagine well enough what was coming, and as he couldn't change the outcome, he may as well get what rest he could. Although the captain had told him not to move from the bed, he probably wouldn't appreciate Cariad soiling it. So he availed himself of the privy, remarking once again how clean everything was. He'd always pictured the Swarm as a filthy people, for no particular reason other than it fit his knowledge of them as being brutal savages. Returning to the bed, he contemplated how he might arrange himself. The pillows at the head were inviting, yet that was too provocative to his mind. So he curled at the foot of it instead and waited for his fate.

* * * *

He must have dozed despite his fear, yet as soon as the door opened again, Cariad became instantly alert. His eyes popped open, giving him a clear view of the captain stepping into the cabin and sliding three bolts into place to lock them in—and everyone else out. The man's gaze flicked to him before he turned up the flame on a hanging lantern, then crossed over to where his trunk sat tied to hooks in the wall to keep it from moving. Without saying a word, the captain stripped off everything he was wearing. The sword and knives went into the trunk, then he sat on it while he removed his tall, leather boots. The rest of his clothing came off, bit by bit, with methodical, unhurried movement. The man paid no attention to Cariad, but it was impossible for him to keep his eyes off the Swarmer.

With the removal of each garment, he was treated to the sight of the most raw, masculine power he'd ever seen. Men everywhere—from the training grounds at his parent's estate to the decks of the Intrepid—had exposed themselves to his gaze with casual regularity. He was no stranger to the sight of men's bodies, and unlike his brother Carwyn, he had never been interested in sneaking peeks. This was different. He couldn't look away. The taut, layered muscle was covered not only by pale skin but with tattoos as well. The Chainer warriors also marked their bodies, but this was different. The Swarm captain's torso, back, arms and legs were dotted with elaborate and colorful pictures of exotic creatures and unfathomable symbols. And when the man turned fully to him, the most startling of all was in full view. His cock—long, thick and fully erect—was wrapped by a red serpent of some kind that started at the root of his dick and ended with the head. How painful had it been to have it etched there, and what did it say about a man who could endure it?

The sight of the tattoo was so startling that he forgot for a moment what the hard cock meant for him. He remembered soon enough when the captain prowled toward the bed with a hooded look. Cariad sat up so quickly that his head swam for a second. He tried to keep his breath even and averted his gaze to gather his courage.

The captain stopped a short distance from the bed, yet close enough that the spicy scent of his skin reached Cariad. "Take off your clothes."

The order was issued with such a quiet and casual tone that Cariad almost didn't comply. Then he remembered that he had no choice in this matter. If he didn't do as told, the Swarmer would simply rip them off his body. Not only would it mean losing his last shred of dignity, but it would also undermine his ruse of being a doxy. "Of course… I was only waiting for you." He was pleased by how steady his voice sounded, although he hadn't quite pulled off any sultriness. With as much grace as he could muster, he started to undress, his clumsy fingers laying waste to his professed eagerness.

It required standing to strip fully. He turned his back to the captain, trying to make it look natural and necessary—and not out of shyness. He folded his clothing, lay them at the foot of the bed and lined his boots up neatly on the floor beside it. A quick glance at the cage told him that at least the monkey wouldn't bear witness to his degradation. The creature sat huddled against one side with her back toward them. *Sleeping, probably.* How long would that last once the sex began? He doubted the captain was a quiet man while taking his pleasure. *Maybe he likes having the monkey watch.* That revolting thought wasn't helping any, so he shoved it aside and with a deep, cleansing breath, he faced the captain. It was hard to resist the urge to hide his nakedness with his arms. As the man scrutinized him, he held a vague hope that his skinny frame and the small cock dangling sadly between his legs might disgust the enormous Swarmer. Surely the man wanted something more alluring in his bed...but no. After a few moments, the man merely went to sit heavily on the side of the bed, his large legs spread open.

The captain crooked a finger at him. "Come." He pointed to the spot between his legs, his meaning clear, even for an untried boy like Cariad.

He made his feet move. What had Carwyn said about cock sucking? *"Delicious."* Well, that might prove to be true, but given the size of the monstrous member, Cariad feared he'd choke to death before he could even form an opinion as to whether sucking a man's dick was enjoyable. It certainly didn't look very appealing, with its prominent veins and slit shiny from what had to be pre-cum.

It was impossible to completely hide his fear and maintain an appearance of an eager whore. *Oh look, a lovely cock to suck. Let me feast on it for your pleasure and mine.* He had no idea if bed-warmers actually talked like that, but he imagined they did. Men's egos being what they were, surely they wanted to be told that their dicks were someone's favorite treat. Try as he might, though, he simply couldn't push those words past his lips. Instead, he tried to convey them with his expression as he entered the V of the captain's legs and slid to his knees. The hardness of the floor was a momentary distraction as he considered his next move.

I should touch him. Yes, that was the next logical move—put his hands on the man's thighs to steady himself and allow some time to adjust to what came next. The Swarmer's skin was warm, smooth and hairless. The tattoos were vivid against it. Cariad slid his fingers up the thighs to rest at the junctures beside the heavy, tight balls. The captain inhaled sharply, and his groin muscles twitched. The reaction was surprisingly pleasing, testament that Cariad could elicit an involuntary response. There was power in that and maybe something he could exploit if he were clever and bold. He dared to move one hand over to first hover by the cock, then lightly clasp the shaft. The hard flesh jumped at the touch, making the serpent appear to move. The captain's breathing became faster, harsher, his chest swelling. The man said nothing and made no move to touch him, yet his demand was easy to read.

Cariad didn't have the luxury to go slowly. If he didn't get on with matters, he might be overpowered and forced to go at a speed and make an effort he wasn't ready for. So, to keep what little control he had, he got on with it, licking his lips and opening his mouth as wide as he could. *I can do this.* The blow job wasn't even the worst of what would happen to him in this cabin. Soon, perhaps even that night, he might look back at this moment and appreciate how easy it was to take this cock into his mouth and not in the other place. His sphincter tightened at the mere thought of being breached. *Don't think about it. Don't think about* anything. *Just do what is necessary.*

Cariad leaned forward and first flicked the Swarmer's cockhead with his tongue, surprised that the taste of the pre-cum didn't disgust him as he'd expected, then pressing his lips over the bulbous flesh. He closed his eyes and took the dick into his mouth, stretching his jaw uncomfortably wide. Even that small part of the cock filled him so completely and instantly that he couldn't swallow much of it. His lungs burned, reminding him to breathe through his nose, while he tried to adjust to accepting something so impossibly big in the relatively small space. He remembered something Carwyn had said about teeth and tried to keep them out of the way as he took more of the heavy cock. His gag reflex kicked in, despite his efforts to suppress it. But when he tried to pull away, the Swarmer beast grabbed his hair to keep him in place. The dick swelled against his tongue, his only warning before cum filled his mouth.

Balto held the Moorcondian boy in position as he flooded him with a release that surprised him with its intensity. It was churlish of him for sure to force the boy to take the cum instead of letting him pull away, but this encounter was about gathering information as much as pleasure. Everything the boy did told him something of importance, and the charmingly awkward blow job was being capped by an obvious inexperience in swallowing cum effectively. He was certain now that this was no whore—not even a bad one. When his balls emptied, he released his grip on the boy's hair and let him slide to the floor, sputtering and coughing, cum dribbling down the corners of his mouth. The newly debauched look was enticing. Balto's cock stirred once more in interest, but he ignored it. There was too much at stake to indulge himself.

Instead, he stood, stepping over his captive and fetching the flask of cider. Tasha had said it needed refilling in the morning but, for the moment, it held enough to be useful. He brought it over to the boy and held it out to him. "Drink this."

The boy's eyes went wide at the command, fear shining through his gaze, but he didn't voice any dissent. He took the flask with obviously shaky hands and downed its contents, wiping at his chin to clean off both the remnants of cum and the cider that had spilled in his haste. He put the container on the floor and stared up at Balto, trying and failing to look sultry. "What now?" The near-squeak in his voice killed any doubt about whether he was eager for more bed sport.

Balto pointed to the bed. "Lie down. I want to…get to know you better." He couldn't help putting as much innuendo into his tone as possible, again to gauge the boy's reaction.

There was a visible shudder, but the Moorcondian proved his mettle by pushing to his feet and climbing onto the bed. After a brief moment of obvious hesitation, the boy lay down on his back. He stared back at Balto, saying nothing, yet there was a challenge in his eyes. "I belong to you now, Captain. Do what you like."

*Oh, very good. I might even believe him...*except he didn't. This boy held secrets, and Balto was sure they would prove vital to his plans and the future of his people. Sitting on the edge of the bed, he perused the boy's body. "I intend to."

Chapter Three

The Moorcondian boy's skin was soft. Balto hadn't felt anything like it since holding Tasha as a baby. He indulged himself by running his fingertips down one arm, across the chest and over to the other side. It was like playing with a delicate toy, not that he'd ever done such a thing. His grandfather and mother hadn't believed in foolish idleness, even for children. Everything he'd done from the moment he'd left the cradle had served a purpose, honing him into a vicious killer. Still, he knew how to be careful, and after a miserable day putting up the necessary front for Mal, killing even when it hadn't been needed, it was calming to simply enjoy the experience of having a pretty boy in his bed. Sex was mostly a quick affair, meeting a need before getting some sleep. This was an indulgence, although one that did serve a purpose—or so he told himself.

The Moorcondian lay mostly still, staring up at the ceiling with a fixed gaze and a blank face. But he couldn't control the entirety of his body. Every stroke by Balto caused the boy's muscles to quiver, and he clenched at the bedding with curled fingers. Some of the reaction was undoubtedly fear. The rest...? He knew the signs of arousal, even if the boy's pretty little cock didn't rise with interest. His breathing hitched, and he licked his lips compulsively. When Balto trailed his fingertips across one of the boy's nipples, the nub hardened into a sharp point, as did the other in a sympathetic reaction. As he slid those fingers down to the flat, smooth belly, a low sound emanated from the boy's throat—part whimper, part moan. The so-close cock swelled a bit—not quite hard, but yet not quite limp, either. Knowing that it was easy to elicit a physical response, even from the unwilling, Balto didn't fool himself into thinking the boy wanted him. Hard as it was, he didn't give into the temptation to take the dick in his clasp. Instead, he retreated to the relatively benign region of the chest.

Time for me to stop playing and get some answers. Balto started out casually. "I thought all Moorcondians were big and hairy—or so I've heard. Sailor gossip is the most unreliable type there is. You lay waste to that assumption. I suppose your smooth, supple skin is something that makes for an appealing whore." When the boy said nothing, he pushed for a response by tweaking one nipple.

His captive hissed, and a flash of anger showed in his expression before he quickly banked it. "Yes." He glanced at Balto. "I'm what every married man at sea wants—someone who reminds him of the wife he's left behind."

Balto couldn't keep the chuckle back. "Are Moorcondian men so delusional that they can fool themselves into thinking you're a woman? Your lips may not give away your sex, but other things clearly do," he added with a flick of his gaze at what lay between the boy's legs.

"It's all small enough to not be noticed, and I'm flat on my face more often than not."

The answer surprised him. Not only was the boy's view of himself far off the mark, but there was also a note of bitterness, as if he pictured himself as nothing more than a couple of holes to fill. And despite the fact that he wasn't what he claimed, it was doubtful he'd ever rolled around with another man to learn such a lesson.

Balto couldn't resist disabusing him of it all. Leaning closer, he said, "Your cock and balls are the perfect size to fit into my mouth, and I much prefer looking at the face of the one I fuck. I'm well aware of how male you are and desire nothing else."

The boy glared up at him. Once more his eyes showed fear but also a hint of something that Balto registered as perhaps desire, which was simply his guilt trying to trick him. He pulled away, forcing himself to stop touching his captive. *Time to get on with what is necessary.* "You're not a whore, so I'll have the truth from you now."

The Moorcondian's eyes widened before he looked away with a sniff. "I'm sorry if I didn't please you. I'm new to the profession, and the Intrepid's captain didn't much care for blow jobs. I'm sure I'll get better with practice," he added while lifting his chin. "Now, if you'd please get on with matters, I'm quite tired after such a long and fretful day."

Balto didn't respond to what amounted to a challenge. It was a brave move to make demands of him, one that could result in being torn to bloody bits and even beaten. He almost did just that, turn the boy over and smack that small ass with the palm of his hand. Violence in response to any insubordination was what he'd been taught. It would be in keeping with the façade he'd adopted as he'd plotted and planned to depose his mother. But no one on the ship, other than perhaps the Moorcondian, expected him to maintain the pretense. That was why they were his crew to begin with. And also, the thought of his hand on the boy's ass was too tempting and might lead him to do more. He needed to have better control over himself.

He stared thoughtfully at the boy. "You would take it that far, wouldn't you—invite the pain and degradation of my violating your innocence to maintain the façade of your story?"

The boy's eyes flashed. "I don't know what you mean. I'm a whore, simply not a very good one, as you've found out for yourself," he added with a grimace. "Do what you want to me. You were going to anyway, regardless of who and what I say I am." There was more of that bitterness in his tone, and fear showed in every quick breath and the clenching of his fingers.

Balto pushed past the sudden urge to gather the boy in his arms and soothe his fears. He tried a different tack. "Cariad. That sounds like a fancy Moorcondian name to me."

"Shows what you know. It's as common as dirt...as am I."

"Hmm." Balto rested his elbow on his knee and his chin on palm. "I suppose then that Moorcondia teaches all its children to speak so elegantly—and feeds everyone food that makes their skin soft and blemish free and their teeth bright and straight." He waited for a response, and when none came, he continued with blunt words. "You are no whore, bad or otherwise. And I'd bet my life that no man has breached your body. Who are you, Cariad? I'll have the truth from you now." He put some meanness into his voice yet wasn't surprised that his captive remained resolute in his story.

"I am who and what I've said. Do with me what you will."

Frustrated, Balto wanted to grab the boy and shake some sense into him. The lie was benefiting no one, but he couldn't be surprised by his captive's stubbornness. Nothing he'd heard or seen had led him to believe that the Moorcondians were anything other than brave and resolute. It was admirable, too, that the boy didn't intend to give him any information that might hurt his people. And the silence itself proved that there was value in having this Moorcondian in his grasp. The time had come for him to take the next and first really dangerous step in his quest to gain control over his people.

"You really would let me cause you agony as I rend your ass rather than tell me the truth. You're either very brave or stupid, and you don't strike me as the latter. Very well, keep your secrets." When he moved to stand, the boy flinched. Balto felt pity and guilt but couldn't afford either sentiment to get in his way. "Slide over to the wall."

He went to lower the flame of the lantern he'd lit. The moonlight streaming through the port holes gave him sufficient light to return to his bed, not that he needed it to find his way. It did, however, give him the ability to see that Cariad huddled against the wall at the far side, gazing back at him. Balto felt suddenly weary and in no mood to utter any reassuring words. Instead, he climbed into bed and flipped the covers over both of them. Then he closed his eyes and dropped into sleep.

* * * *

Cariad woke surprisingly refreshed after a deep sleep. As he fluttered his eyes open, he half expected his body to be in pain from a rough usage. Except for a slight ache in his jaw, however, nothing hurt or even hinted that the captain had somehow abused him during the night. The idea that he'd even sleep through such abuse was ridiculous, of course, unless he'd been drugged after all. He felt no hint of that, either. His mind was clear, and except for the memories of the terror of the previous day, plus some remnants of disturbing dreams filled with erotic images, he had a renewed determination to survive his predicament. There was one problem with his body, though, that he detected as he started to sit up. His damn cock was hard, the pathetic thing looking for attention that he rarely gave it. What was the point? He found his pleasure in being useful. That was enough for him.

Fortunately, he remained covered with the soft blanket the captain had settled him under. It hid his unruly state, allowing him to keep track of his captor as he dressed for the day. The man had left the bed without disturbing him, which was a surprise in itself. And now he stood by his chest, dressing himself in the same garb as he'd been in the day before. Seeing him put clothing on was almost as interesting as seeing him take them off. He remained the most impressive example of the male species Cariad had ever clapped eyes on. It was a bothersome truth, yet he couldn't stop watching.

When he'd strapped his sword belt onto his waist, the captain turned to stare back at him. He smiled. "Did you sleep well?"

Cariad dropped his gaze. "It's a comfortable bed."

With a chuckle, the man strode over to him and whipped the blanket off before Cariad could even squawk with indignation. "Harder still to miss that you're a boy now, hmm?" His gaze was leveled directly at Cariad's groin.

He tugged the blanket back in place. "That's from my full bladder."

The Swarmer laughed and shook his head. "A pity. If you were interested, I would be happy to return your favor from last night." He walked to the door, snapping his finger. "Pia, come." The monkey launched herself from the cage, using pieces of furniture to leverage herself onto his shoulder. "Tasha will be here soon with your breakfast and water to wash with."

Cariad stayed where he was, not daring to use the privy for fear that the girl would enter while he walked naked back to the bed. He didn't attempt to use the blanket as a covering, either, knowing it would drag on the floor, and he wanted to wash before putting his own clothing back on. He didn't have long to wait, the door opening again soon after the captain had shut it. Tasha beamed a smile at him as she entered, her arms laden with a bigger basket and a bowl of water that she set on the small table by the side of the bed.

"Good morning, Cariad." She put the basket beside the bowl. "Is it okay for me to use your name? The captain said it was because you are only a whore—one step up from a slave, so not to worry about showing deference."

The girl spoke the insulting words as if they held no more import than the reporting of the state of the weather. Cariad figured that was the captain's way of poking at him. He wasn't about to fall prey to such a ploy and didn't want to take out his ire on the slave girl anyway. "It's fine."

She smiled again and patted the basket. "I have your breakfast in here, as well as a cloth for washing and something for you to wear today." She then swept up the tunic, trousers and small clothes he'd dropped the previous evening. "I will see that these are washed."

"That isn't necessary." He hated to think of a slave tending to such a chore for him. On the Intrepid, men were paid to work in the laundry. Here he had to assume it was a slave's job, and he didn't want to add to their burden. Not to mention Tasha had said she did that chore for the captain and he wasn't going to risk making her day any harder, especially given how kind she'd been. "I'll take care of them myself."

"Ha! What a funny thing to say." She went to the door. "I'll be back to clean up."

With that, she left the cabin, leaving Cariad open-mouthed and perplexed. He didn't know what to make of his situation. On the one hand, the captain treated him as a whore—mostly. And on the other, Tasha at least acted as if he were the man's guest. It confused him, but as there was no way to figure out the minds of the Swarmers as yet, he took advantage of the privacy to relieve himself, eat, wash and dress. The clothing he'd been given was surprisingly small, and he would have worried that they were part of Tasha's undoubtedly limited wardrobe, except they looked more like what the captain and his crew wore than the slave's attire. The trousers hugged his legs and were made of a soft brown leather. The tunic was a shade lighter and long enough that it hit just above his knees. All of it smelled like the spice he'd detected in the ship and its crew, as did his skin. It must be a scent infused into their soap. His own belt pulled the extra cloth up some and his boots hid the material bagging around his ankles.

Once he'd taken care of the necessities, he stood with his hands on his hips, wondering how he would spend the rest of his day. Now that he knew his captor wasn't prone to immediate cruelty, he wasn't as afraid as he'd been when first brought onboard. He told himself that it was foolish not to be terrified every second, yet with his belly full of warm oatmeal and dried meat, he couldn't quite work up those feelings. Instead, he considered boredom to be the next problem to face. He eyed the desk drawer where the captain had stashed his writing desk and wondered if he dared retrieve it.

"It's mine. I can take it back if I want." So he did, and, sitting cross-legged on the bed, he began to do that which had always brought him joy and solace.

* * * *

As usual, Cariad had become so absorbed by his drawing that time passed without notice. It surprised him when Tasha returned with her usual cheer. Yet another basket swung from her arm. "Time for your midday meal." She leaned in on tiptoes to look at his paper. "Oh, what an amazing likeness of the captain."

Cariad quickly slid the drawing into the desk and tried to hide his embarrassment. "He has an interesting face." True as that was, he hadn't consciously intended to draw the man. It had just happened, and he couldn't stop. Tasha was seeing only the latest sketch. He'd done two others, working meticulously to capture the man's image and hadn't been satisfied with his efforts the first two times. And there was an aborted drawing of the man's snake tattoo, but once he realized what he was doing, he'd ripped it up and tossed it down the privy.

"If that's another way of saying he's gorgeous, I agree." She swapped the new basket out for the old one. "Come and eat. I have orders to bring you on deck once you're done."

The thought of leaving the cabin excited him before worry set in. "What for? I mean, why am I going up there?" Sliding off the bed, he returned his writing desk to the drawer.

"I have no idea. My master doesn't explain himself to me."

"Yes, of course." Cariad returned to the bed and peered into the basket of food. There was a jug of cider, bread, cheese and dried fruit. He tucked into it all with gusto, trying not to be unnerved by Tasha watching him.

"Is the captain good in bed?"

Cariad choked on his mouthful of food and washed it down with some cider before responding. "What kind of a question is that?"

The girl shrugged. "I'm curious, that's all...about sex," she clarified needlessly. "No one else on this ship would ever speak of such things to me, so I thought I'd ask you. And being a whore, you must talk about it all the time and know when a man does sex well."

"Does sex well?" Cariad shook his head as if to toss the words out of his mind. "You are too young to ask such a thing...or talk about sex." He inwardly winced at how much he sounded like a prudish aunt.

Tasha sat down beside him, her eyes alight. "If I don't ask, how am I to learn? And if I'm too young to hear about it, you're too young to do it."

"I'm a grown man," he countered, trying not to be defensive about his unimpressive appearance.

Tasha peered at him closely. "Barely." She sighed. "Anyway, you haven't answered my question about how the captain was."

"Nor will I ever," he replied as sternly as he could.

Tasha only sighed. "I sometimes dream about being in this bed with him myself. But the captain only likes boys, not girls—and even if he wanted me, he'd never take me because again, my papa would be very cross about it."

Cariad still couldn't believe that a slave would be able to show anger toward a free person, but he held his tongue because he didn't want the topic of sex to keep going. When he'd finished his meal, he repacked the basket and slung it over his arm. "You said something about my going on deck?"

"Yes, of course." Tasha hopped off the bed and held her hand out to take the basket from him.

"No. I'll carry this. You have the one from breakfast to deal with."

"You're very sweet. Are all Moorcondian whores like that?" Something about the look in her eye told him she was deliberately gauging his reaction.

Whatever game was being played to make him confess who he really was, he wasn't going to take the bait. "Yes. We have to be to lure men into giving us money."

With a knowing smile, the girl led him out of the cabin and down the hallway away from the stairs leading up to the deck. "If you are going to be helpful with the food, we will go to the galley first."

They passed a couple of sailors on the way, and what surprised Cariad was not how they paid him no mind, but it was the easy kindness they showed Tasha. There was no leering or pawing at her. Instead, they gave her room to pass and even greeted her with friendly nods. It didn't make sense to him. The Swarm were a vicious people. He'd seen that already himself. A slave should be nothing to them except a source of labor and occasional fun. Maybe they acted the way they did for the same reason that they treated him as if he didn't exist—to avoid courting the ire of the captain by impinging on what was his.

The galley brought out even more questions. The cook was obviously a Swarmer, given how he looked, and there was no slave mark that he could see. And yet the man smiled at Tasha and took the basket from her so that she could take the one Cariad carried in turn. The dirty items ended up in the hands of a Chainer boy who was even younger than Tasha. He did have the tattoo that proclaimed him as belonging to the captain. He'd undoubtedly been captured on one of the Swarm's raids. And while he wasn't as cheery as Tasha, he didn't appear afraid, either. There was no mark of violence on him, and he looked healthy enough.

This ship and its crew were getting curiouser and curiouser, the captain most of all. Before he could ponder it further, Tasha took him by the hand and led him back down the passageway and up the stairs to the deck. The sun had passed its zenith, but the day was still warm. All around him the Swarmers went about their business, as competent and dedicated as any of the sailors he'd observed on the Intrepid. Tasha tugged him along to the pilot house. There, the captain stood with braced legs steering the vessel. Even the back of him was impressive, a fact that irked Cariad, yet the sentiment rose unbidden in his mind.

"Here is your Moorcondian whore, Captain." Tasha gave him a little push forward, then raced away.

The man looked over his shoulder at him. There was an obvious hunger in his gaze. Then he shouted. "Amadeus!"

A man, as big and muscular as any Cariad had seen so far, pushed past him and went to the captain. "Sir?"

"Take the wheel."

Once he'd been relieved, the Swarmer captain approached Cariad and grabbed him by the waist. Before he knew what was happening, he landed on the man's lap as he sat down on a nearby bench.

The captain hugged him close. "You're so stiff, darling boy. One would think you don't like my touch. Surely you've learned to at least pretend you enjoy cuddling with whomever has bought your body."

"You didn't buy it. You stole it." The words were out of his mouth before he could stop them.

The Swarmer laughed. "See how lucky I am with my new toy, Amadeus? He's got a bit of a sting."

"Better than lying there like a wet rag, I imagine, sir." The man steering the ship didn't bother to look at them as he spoke. Small mercies that Cariad's humiliation wasn't being scrutinized.

Still, he knew he wasn't helping his cause by being so prickly. So he forced himself to loosen up in the man's hold and even rested his head against the broad chest. "My apologies, Captain Balthazar. I shouldn't be so churlish. You've been very generous."

"Hmm." The man put his face close to Cariad and sniffed loudly. "You smell like us now."

"Tasha was kind enough to bring me soap."

"Kindness had nothing to do with it. I ordered her to, and Tasha is a very biddable girl."

Cariad managed to bite back what he was thinking, that Tasha deserved to be free. "As I said, you've been good to me." He forced himself to splay his hand against the chest, trying to make it a coy gesture. "I'm happy to service you, Captain Balthasar."

"Call me Balto." He tugged Cariad's hair free from the simple braid he had put it in after washing up. "And I prefer this to be loose." He threaded his fingers through the strands, the feel of it a gentle caress. "It's pleasing to the eye in the sunlight." Then he tightened his grip, much as he'd done the night before, and tipped Cariad's head back.

The man's stare was unnerving, and his lips were so close to Cariad's that, for a moment, he thought the man was going to kiss him. When he didn't, there was a second of disappointment, which made him mad at himself. *I've never wanted to be kissed before. Why would I want this man to be the first?* He didn't. That was the truth of it—or so he insisted to his own mind and felt relief when he was let go.

The captain stood, putting Cariad in front of him and embracing him with his long arms around Cariad's waist. "Do these waters look familiar?"

"I don't know. Should they, Balto?" He deliberately used the man's name as he'd been told to do. It was critical that he do better in his role of a doxy.

The Swarmer didn't respond, but the answer came anyway. There was an island dotting the horizon, and even at a distance, he recognized it. That was part of what made him such an excellent cartographer. He saw all things and remembered every detail. The Intrepid had passed this way not two days ago. "There's no one left to attack there." He didn't try to hide his anger. He was pretending to be a bed-warmer, not a heartless bastard. "You've destroyed or taken anyone and anything of value already."

The man was quiet for a while and even heaved a sigh. "We're not going to the island but past it."

Startled by the news, Cariad tried to turn around to face the man. Balto kept him in place. "You're heading farther into the Southern Chains' waters?" It was a bold move, given that as far as he could tell, there were other islands to plunder circling the perimeter of the waters in which the Chainers routinely sailed.

"I am and will go as far as necessary to run into a Chainer ship—or a Moorcondian one. It doesn't matter either way."

"You're a fool for doing so. Any ship you encounter will be a warship manned with seasoned warriors. It won't be easy pickings like the Intrepid and those poor villagers were. It took you two ships as it was to be victorious, and now you have only this one." It was stupid to point it all out. If nothing else, he now had a better chance of surviving his captivity and being returned to the safety of the main island of the Chainers. He should be delighted to hear this news, yet there was instead a nameless dread sneaking into his belly.

"You'd be right if I intended to wage war on the first ship I see. I don't."

Cariad worked to understand what the man meant. "If you're not going to attack, what are you going to do?"

"Talk."

Chapter Four

"How did your night go, Balto?"

Balto didn't spare Amadeus a glance, keeping his gaze on the ocean, willing a ship to appear over the horizon. "As well as the last four."

Amadeus snorted. "Not well, then. How blue are your balls now?"

"About as deep a shade as yours are going to be when I kick them."

"I retract my needling, sir, with the humblest of apologies." The man's tone implied otherwise. The entire crew no doubt knew that he spent each night beside a fuckable boy and was doing no such thing. Amadeus was simply close enough to him to get away with the ribbing.

"He is stubborn," he offered with a sigh. "He keeps up the tale of being a doxy, not taking the bait no matter how often I or others refer to him as a whore. I'm sure he's a nobleman, which is perfect for my plans, but lying next to such a fetching boy does try my patience each night."

"You could press the matter more forcefully."

Balto dismissed the idea with a quick shake of his head. "No. If I abuse him further, my plans will be in jeopardy. There is only so much insult the Moorcondians will tolerate, but I believe the boy can be co-opted to our cause—his being more so with every moment he spends on this ship. Tasha says he's respectful of her, and she in turn gives away tidbits of what life is like as my slave. I hope it gives him a good impression of me, to some extent."

He left out how the boy also sketched pictures of him daily—not of the crew or the ship or anything else that could be of strategic value—only him. And they were flattering images to be sure, as he'd made a point of looking at them each morning before the boy woke. He wondered if the boy acknowledged, even to himself, that he was intrigued by his Swarmer captor. The pictures alluded to it, as did the way his breath hitched when Balto climbed into bed to lie beside him. Then there was the way his dick woke hard, something the boy tried to hide. Perhaps it was his bladder driving that reaction, but that didn't explain how sometimes while deep in sleep, the boy rolled toward him and nestled against his side. That occurrence certainly woke Balto and tortured him as if he were being interrogated in his mother's dungeon.

Amadeus clapped him on the back. "I know how important it is that we succeed here, and I can appreciate the fact that your captive may prove very useful. But we are ready to move without any help, as we've always been. This new twist of yours isn't necessary, and you aren't going to wish a ship to appear by staring out at the ocean most of the day."

Something flickered in the distance, nothing he could make out, yet his heart sped up. "I wouldn't be so sure of that."

* * * *

Given the speed at which the two ships approached each other, Balto estimated that they would be within hailing distance before nightfall. He'd ordered the white flag to be flown as soon as he'd identified what he'd seen, so that regardless of the timing, the Chainer ship would know that they meant to talk, not fight. At least he hoped they would understand that intent. If it were him captaining that vessel, he'd expect a trap. The Chainers weren't dumb and certainly not the one he was sure captained that particular ship. Through the spyglass, he'd seen the numbered markings on its flag in the way of Chainers, and that told him it was their top warrior, Kai Aleki, sailing toward him.

It was the best of luck, because the man would have the authority to make a deal. They wouldn't have to wait to find him. Of course, based on the man's reputation, it wasn't surprising that he led the way for his prima kailisa's fleet. Balto would expect no less, and again, based on what he'd heard, he believed the man would be open to bargaining. Only people like his brother were quick to fight first and ask questions later with a sword at the enemies' necks. And if he could convince Cariad of his sincerity, the chance of success would improve significantly. Amadeus had been right that they didn't need outsiders in order to prevail in their coup, but it would be damn helpful if they had it.

He entered his cabin to find the boy sitting cross-legged on the bed with his writing desk across his lap.

Surprisingly, Pia sat beside him, grooming herself. He hadn't realized his pet had warmed up to his captive and vice versa. They both stopped what they were doing and stared at him as he stood contemplating how he felt about this homey scene. Pia went right back to picking and washing herself, uninterested in his arrival and certainly unconcerned by it.

Cariad's reaction was different. The boy stuck the sheet of paper he'd been drawing on into the desk and slammed it shut, as he always did when Balto arrived back in the cabin. "Is something wrong? You did say I could pass the time this way during the day, did you not?" His tone and expression were defiant. "Are you looking for me to give you…pleasure?"

"No, I am not." Balto shut the door and leaned against it. "Do you think me so meanspirited that I would deny you the pleasure of what you enjoy in order to service me on a whim?" *Even though you silently deny me every damn night.*

The boy shrugged and averted his gaze. "Swarmers have proven themselves to be vicious in everything. Why should you be any different about the use of my body?"

Balto waited a beat before responding, counseling himself to be patient. "A fair point. As it happens, however, I am—different, that is, from my mother and brother and those who follow them. I want something better for my people."

"Well, massacring villagers isn't going to accomplish that."

"I agree." Pushing away from the door, he went to sit beside the boy, displacing Pia, who with a chitter of annoyance climbed onto his shoulder. "I see that you and Pia have become friends."

Cariad rolled his eyes. "We've come to an understanding. She lets me draw her and I don't mind her sitting close to me. You said she was clean, and that is true—more than I am these days."

"You'd like a bath, no doubt. You may soon get your wish," he added.

"I don't want some poor slaves to lug a bathtub in here and fill it with water."

"That's good, because we have no such thing for them to carry or fill. I bet there's one on the Chainer ship heading this way, however."

Hope flared into the boy's eyes, then died. "You're going to attack it."

"No. I told you I wanted to talk, and I do. Even now, we are flying a white flag. Do you think the Chainers will honor its meaning?"

"They might if they think it's sincere. If it's a trap, they'll be looking out for that. It won't be easy to lure them in."

"Agreed. That is why I'm bringing you up top. Their lookout should spy you easily enough."

Tossing the writing desk onto the bed, the boy lurched to his feet with fists at his side. "I will *not* let you use me as bait!" His chest rose and fell with rapid breaths.

Balto stood up slowly so as not to aggravate him more. Nevertheless, Pia leaped off him with a screech of annoyance. He paid her no mind and kept his gaze on the Moorcondian. "I want to display you as an incentive for them to not…overreact to our presence."

"Not fire first, you mean, so that you can. They have nothing but arrows to lob at you, so you should feel confident about victory." His bitterness hung in the air between them.

Compared to his brother, Balto was a pillar of patience, but it was hard not to shake the boy with frustration. Any type of violence, no matter how minor, was the wrong way to make his point. He knew that and called upon the calm that he'd learned to instill in himself. "I'm *not* going to give the order to attack, even if they rain arrows down on us. If peace is to be secured, someone has to take the first step to demonstrate a commitment to it, despite the possibility of death."

Those words had the right effect. At least it caused Cariad to be quiet. He studied Balto for a few seconds before speaking again. "You can't mean you want to negotiate a treaty with the Chainers."

"I do mean it. I want to cease my people's aggression against everyone, including the Chainers and the Moorcondians."

Cariad's eyes narrowed before he barked out a laugh. "You forget that I've seen what you do and have met your brother. The two of you disputed who would take possession of me. Hardly a gesture of goodwill."

"I never said my family was onboard with what I want. To increase the likelihood of my success, I have come to realize that I must convince your people to help me depose my mother…and dispatch my brother, as well." Although Balto had rarely spoken the words out loud, he knew that the only way he could bring about peace was to first destroy what was left of his family.

"You're planning a coup?"

"Yes."

They stared at each other for a long time, Cariad obviously brooding over things and Balto doing his best to show he meant what he'd said. Finally, he added what he believed was further proof of his sincerity. "I know you weren't the doxy of the Intrepid's captain.

Your behavior toward me proves that. And I would like to think that my treatment of you demonstrates my honorable intentions. You are of noble birth, yet not an officer of that ship. You draw exceedingly well. The only possible reason for you to be out at sea is that you are a cartographer." Before the boy could argue that he was not, Balto held up his hand. "There is no point in denying it or for us to even discuss this further. Come onto the deck, and I'll show you I mean what I say."

He clasped the boy firmly by the arm before he could evade his touch or say more. It didn't take much effort to get him up onto the deck. The sight of the Chainer ship's approach was easily seen now without the need of a spyglass.

Cariad stiffened at first, then wrenched out of his grasp to race to stand by the railing. "That's Kai Aleki's ship." He slammed his hand over his own mouth.

Balto went to stand behind him. "Don't worry. You haven't given anything away. I recognized that it's the leader of the Chainers' flotilla from its flag. Do you know the kai?"

"No."

Balto could tell the boy was lying. The way he'd said the warrior's name told Balto differently. And any type of acquaintance between the Chainer captain and this Moorcondian nobleman could prove very useful. If nothing else, it meant they wouldn't be fired upon without provocation. He wasn't leading his men to certain death. If only the same could be said for him…

* * * *

Cariad was surprised that his ordeal seemed to be coming to a joyful end—and quickly at that. From where he sat in the dinghy, Aleki's ship quickly got closer as Balto rowed them toward it with long, quick strokes. The white flag had been honored by the Chainers, and it hadn't been a trap, either. Through semaphore communication that was unintelligible to him yet a method used by both Moorcondia and the Chainers that the Swarm had picked up, Balto had asked for a face-to-face meeting with Aleki. The Chainer warrior had agreed, so long as it was on his ship and Cariad had to be brought along. He wouldn't have thought Balto so foolish as to agree, but he had. His explanation was simple. He'd never intended to use Cariad as a hostage, merely capitalized upon his capture as being extra security that the Chainers or the Moorcondians would hear him out. He'd told Cariad only a little of his plan to overthrow his mother—really nothing at all, other than a general intent to do so. Cariad was keen to learn the details of what the man proposed, although he dared not hope that the Swarmer's offer of a truce and treaty was sincere or that it would end the Swarm's attacks. It was too good to be true. There could easily be some complex part of the man's plan that involved using the Swarm's enemies for help with the intention of turning on them after the fact. That kind of duplicitous behavior made perfect sense to him.

Still, here was Balto, rowing himself unarmed to his possible death, as far as he knew. Aleki wasn't going to simply let him go, nor his ship without a fight, unless he believed that Balto was serious and capable of carrying out his purported plot against his own mother and brother, not to mention untold numbers of his people who must be loyal to them. If nothing else, however, the Swarmer was demonstrating amazing courage with an outer calm that Cariad doubted he could muster if the positions were reversed. Even now, they were in range of the archers lined along the side of the ship, ready to let loose at the first provocation. Cariad was sure he was safe from a stray arrow, given the skill of the Chainer warriors. But as the target, Balto would not be so lucky. For some reason, the thought of the man being in such mortal danger disturbed him.

He couldn't help blurting out his worry. "What's to stop the kai from killing you the moment you step onboard his ship? Will you use me as a shield?" That thought had popped up unbidden and was the only thing that made sense.

Balto cocked an eyebrow at him. "What a foolish plan that would be. You're too small to make an effective shield against arrows or swords. A good swing would lop off my head without ruffling your hair."

Cariad winced at the cold observation. The man had a point, though. Their height difference was significant. "Why are you taking this risk? The kai wants me back, of course, but it doesn't mean he intends to actually listen to what you have to say. Why didn't you leave me as a hostage on your ship to force his hand?"

"As I've already said, you're not a hostage. I never intended you to be, only an incentive. And, regardless, I would have never allowed Malachi to get his brutal hands on you," he added surprisingly.

"You let him take Sean."

"Needs must. I can't save everybody…unless and until I am victorious. Intercepting a Chainer or Moorcondian ship was always my intent when I left my home this last time," he continued after a look of sadness flashed across his violet eyes—or maybe that was simply moonlight. "Acquiring you was pure luck."

"You could have told me this from the start." The fact that the man hadn't confided in him, had forced him to pretend to be something that he wasn't, to suck his cock... Well, that hadn't been quite the miserable chore he'd expected. Still, it was an intolerable deception. Aleki would have the man's head for that afront alone, not that Cariad intended to speak of what he'd done. It was embarrassing, and besides, if there was a hope for peace, he didn't want to be the one to squash it.

"And you had every chance of telling me who you really were."

Cariad huffed and crossed his arms. "That was different. As far as I knew, you intended to enslave me. That last thing I wanted was to hand you any leverage against my people."

"Fair point. Not that I know the full truth of your identity even now, but it matters not. I'm handing you back to your ally. I'm sure you'll be home in no time."

Cariad doubted that very much. There was no way Aleki would turn his ship around simply to drop Cariad off at the safest harbor. He was one man and not important in the larger scheme of things. Plus, he still intended to help the war effort with his cartography skills. Nothing had changed that. Of course, while Balto had his suspicions, he didn't know for sure what role Cariad had served on the Intrepid.

There was no more opportunity to talk in any event, as Balto's long and strong arms brought them quickly to Aleki's ship. A rope ladder had been lowered over the side. Balto tied the dinghy to it then gestured for Cariad to climb up. If there had been any doubt about the man's intent where he was concerned, that gesture laid it to rest. Cariad knew that as soon as he stepped foot on deck, the Chainers would surround him to provide a protective barrier. He would be truly free of Balto's control. And he was right... Aleki himself helped him over the railing and embraced him for a moment before shoving him behind his line of warriors.

Balto was seized the moment he cleared the railing, archers still at the ready, while warriors searched his body with rough hands. The man stood unresisting through it all with his gaze somehow peering over and around the Chainers to find Cariad. The scrutiny should have been unnerving, and he should have felt nothing but relief. Instead, he was a bundle of nerves, almost as severe as when he'd first been taken by the Swarmers. And although it irked him on many levels to feel that way, he knew it was out of concern for Balto's safety, which was the worst reason of all. He shouldn't care about the man's fate. *Why do I?*

When the search of Balto had finished, two Chainers held him by the arms against the railing while Aleki stepped forward and stood with his legs braced and his hands on his hips. He somehow managed to look down at Balto, despite the fact that the Swarmer was a good head taller than he. "I am Kai Aleki."

Balto gave him a slight grin. "I know. I am Balthazar, son of Lilith, suzerain of the Swarm. I thank you for permitting me to board."

"I've heard of you. They call you the Bloodletter and your brother, Malachi, the Destroyer. For good reason, I assume."

Balto sighed. "I won't deny it. Mal and I have been under my mother's control for a long time. Before that, our grandfather forged us. They both wanted to make killers of me and my brother. They succeeded longer than I would have wished with me—and completely with Malachi. I can't change the past, but I'm here to make a different future for myself and my people."

"You've returned my brother by marriage, so that alone belies your reputation and was reason enough for me to agree to this meeting."

Balto's smile broadened. "I knew Cariad for a nobleman from the start. He insisted that he was something quite different. It never occurred to me that he is a relative of yours, however." He left it at that, and Cariad was grateful for it.

"How did he come to be on your ship? What has happened to the Intrepid?"

When Balto hesitated, a look of sorrow on his face, Cariad decided it was time for him to become part of the discussion and not merely a topic of it. He muscled his way past his protectors and went to Aleki's side. "It was attacked and destroyed by two Swarmer ships, Captain Balthazar's and his brother's. This man saved me from certain slavery."

"I'm not surprised by the news about the Intrepid but am surprised by your treatment." Aleki looked at him. "Ambrose?"

"Captured, as were many of the crew along with him," Cariad shared.

"He will be sacrificed to the God of Blood," Balto interjected, doing himself no favors. "There is no hope of rescuing him, but if you hear me out, I have a way to free the others and stop this mad aggression my people are waging against yours."

"What reason is there for me to believe you?"

"There is none, other than the fact that I have returned Cariad to you and stand here at your mercy. I have no agenda other than a desire to bring about peace. Will you listen to me?"

Aleki didn't answer right away. He stared at Balto for long seconds before nodding once. "I see no harm in it now that you are here. Come… We will speak in my ready room." He turned to Cariad. "I will have you brought to my cabin so that you might bathe and rest."

Cariad didn't hesitate to nix that idea. "With all due respect, kai, I am part of this and deserve to hear what Balto has to say."

Aleki gave him a curious look. "Balto?"

"It's what he prefers to be called," Cariad explained, trying not to sound defensive or make a big deal out of it. "I may not be a warrior, but I do serve at the command of my king."

Aleki barked out a laugh. "So like my wife. Very well, come on then."

They very quickly ended up sitting at a large wooden table, Balto literally at sword point. The man showed no indication that he was the least bit disturbed with his precarious position. At Aleki's gesture, he began to make his case.

"I shall start with who the people of the Swarm are. I'm sure you are curious, and it will hopefully help you understand what I intend to do." He took a deep breath and let it out slowly. His gaze focused on a distant point as he spoke. "For many generations, longer than any of us know, my people were nomadic, traveling from island to island. Some were traders. Others settled down to farm and make crafts—weaving, throwing pots and the like—for use and more trading. Still others made their way by pirating. There was near-constant conflict among various groups, the strong preying on the weak, as they always do, and no central leadership to bring order to any of them…until my grandfather.

"After growing up in a pirating family, he settled on land to become an alchemist. What he understood about compounds allowed him to dazzle people, trick them into thinking he had magical powers. He was also a charismatic man, although I never found him so. Many people started following him as a knower of all things. Then he found a way to enhance the chemicals you use for your pretty fireworks. My people suddenly had a weapon far more advanced than anyone in the known world."

Aleki stopped him. "What is this you say? What weapon?"

Cariad spoke up. "I've seen it and now understand how they are able to decimate those they attack so easily. They shoot iron balls from the sides of their ships. It's horrific," he added with a grimace.

"Just so," Balto confirmed.

Aleki rounded on him. "So this is a trap after all. Your ship can lob those balls at us at any time."

"They can but they won't. If you kill me, they have orders to flee. If you pursue them, they have orders to fire upon you only so much as necessary to make their escape. And regardless, I can and will provide you with the formula, so that you can achieve the same explosive power for your own ships."

There was a stunned silence, then Aleki asked the obvious question. "Why would you betray your people like that?"

Balto spread his arms with the limited movement afforded him. "It was my grandfather who betrayed my people, and now my mother and brother continue his bloodthirsty ways. This is the only chance my people have to reclaim an honorable and peaceful life."

Aleki sat back. "So you are in this alone?"

"No. My crew was carefully picked by me, based on their like-minded views. And there are others in the citadel from which my mother rules as the suzerain of our race. Once we make the move to overthrow her, I believe there are many more who will support us. My grandfather ruled by convincing others that he'd been visited by the God of Blood and shown the path for our peoples' future by teaching him the very formula he'd devised on his own. For him, it was a means to an end, one big con filled with the showmanship he did so well. The sacrifices he eventually started to perform were to enthrall the masses and control them with terror—a means to an end that he once told me was an unpleasant and tedious chore, as if the horror and pain he inflicted was nothing more than a boring task. That was bad enough. My mother and brother, however, are motivated not just by greed but with a lust for violence. She loves to plunge the knife into her victims to tear out their hearts and guts. You can see the madness in her eyes, and it's only going to get worse. It must stop."

"So your plan is to give us a chance to fight at their level."

Balto shook his head. "The formula is a goodwill gesture. What I hope to do is put an end to this long before you outfit your ship."

Aleki eyed him with renewed skepticism. "With our help?"

"Yes. I need your ships—as many as you can spare—to congregate around the citadel but stay out of sight. I will give you the coordinates, and once the coup begins, we will light the sky with fireworks as a signal for you to come join us."

Aleki snorted. "Now *that* sounds like a trap."

"I understand. That's why I'm giving you the formula. I used to help my grandfather in his laboratory, so I had to learn it whether I wanted to or not. No matter what else happens, you will have the means to mount an effective defense if you pass it to your comrades before making your journey to the citadel."

"If it works."

"Surely you have men onboard who can assess its efficacy."

"Hmm," was all Aleki said, nodding to one of his men who left the cabin. "We'll need more than such simple instructions."

"Naturally. I'll give you everything in detail, including a map of the waters around the island where the citadel is located, as well as that of the city itself." He looked right at Cariad. "I'm sure such a talented cartographer can make sense of all that."

Cariad folded his arms and glared back. "I never said I was any such thing."

Now Balto grinned in a way that made Cariad want to slap the look off his face. "No, you said you were a whore."

Ignoring the gasps of the men around him, Cariad said, "Stop using that word. I hate it."

"I know you do. That's why I had everyone call you it. I wanted to see if it would goad you into telling the truth." He switched his attention to Aleki. "You should know that Cariad equipped himself admirably."

"I would expect nothing less from a lord of Kenworth—if his brother, my wife, is any indication."

A calculating look entered Balto's eyes. "You married a man?"

"For the sake of a treaty between the Southern Chain and Moorcondia, yes."

"Interesting… Perhaps then you'll understand that I will need something more personal from you…men, warriors that I can claim I've captured and Cariad, the captive my brother already knows I have. It should deflect my family from any suspicions about what I've been doing."

Sliding his chair back suddenly, Aleki jumped to his feet and leaned over with his palms flat on the tabletop. "Warriors, perhaps. Cariad, *never*."

Balto didn't so much as flinch at the aggressive posture. "Well, I suppose I could claim that the boy fell overboard or that I killed him in a fit of unbridled passion. They might believe I let myself lose such a valuable prize."

The heated look he sent Cariad across the table caused his heartbeat to speed up, and the cabin suddenly felt very warm.

Aleki pointed a finger at the Swarmer captain. "Yes, that. Make up whatever story you wish, but Cariad is *not* going back to your ship, let alone accompany you to the seat of the Swarm's power, far from any rescue I could mount to save him."

Cariad should have been reassured by the kai's words, yet he wasn't. Having spent the last several days hoping to escape Balto and go back to helping his people map out the Swarm's waters, he wasn't so sure that his cartography skills were the most effective way for him to serve. He dared to speak up. "Your pardon, kai, but I would like to hear what Captain Balto proposes. If having me with him would help our cause…"

Aleki rounded on him, looking fierce, and spoke to him with a stern tone he'd never heard before. "No. It is *not* your decision, and there is no point in your hearing more." He gestured toward a young warrior. "Escort Lord Cariad to my cabin and see that he is made comfortable."

Incensed at being dismissed as if he were a recalcitrant child, he wanted to stomp his foot as if he were one. He looked at Balto, although why he thought he'd find an ally there was hard to fathom. The Swarmer simply shrugged. There was no help from that quarter, even though the plan they all spoke about originated with him. When Cariad opened his mouth to plead his case with the kai once more, the Chainer gave him a look that conveyed how foolish it would be to gainsay him. No wonder Carwyn said the man could be irritatingly high-handed when the mood struck. Understanding, however, that the captain of the ship had to be obeyed, Cariad stood and left the cabin before one of the warriors could carry him away. He had no doubt that was the next command Aleki would give.

He needed to bide his time and plead his case later, because the more he thought about it, the more he was convinced that sailing into the mouth of the enemy might be his destiny after all.

Chapter Five

Balto was grateful that he was both still alive and being fed a quite delicious meal. After he'd laid out his plan, the kai had agreed to allow him to step onto the deck long enough to show his crew that he yet lived. Now he was being treated more as a guest, which really only meant that the warriors surrounding him weren't holding the points of their swords at his neck, although they stood at the ready if he so much as twitched the wrong way. He ignored them because in the kai's place he would do the same. It was enough for the moment that the Chainers were considering joining forces with him. He really couldn't ask for anything more.

Perhaps one thing.

He knew better than to inquire after Cariad. While he'd known the boy was from an elevated position in his country, he hadn't imagined that he'd be related to the kai by marriage. The connection was both a help and a hindrance. The boy had been instrumental in the kai's willingness to listen to him, he was certain of it. But the Chainer was also too emotional when it came to protecting Cariad. Convincing Aleki to give the boy back to him would be difficult, notwithstanding that the boy himself seemed to pick up the wisdom of it immediately. The fact that having him with him again was pleasing on a personal level didn't signify. What mattered was deposing his mother and destroying his brother's power before he could become her successor.

"I will have to kill them both," he said more to himself than the kai, who sat across from him, eating as well.

"The suzerain and the Destroyer? Of course. If not, they will remain a danger to any new government you form. No amount of captivity will neutralize their influence and ambition."

Balto sighed and took a long swig of the Chainers' most excellent wine. "Yes. I understood that the moment I decided to do this thing."

"Hard for you."

Balto flashed on memories of how they'd both brutalized him when he proved to be less blood thirsty than they. He hated them, and no familial tie would change that. Still… "Yes, it will be, but I will do what's necessary." He sat back and toyed with his cup. "I appreciate your hearing me out and considering agreeing to my plan."

"But?" The kai was no fool.

"But, I would ask you to reconsider your position about Cariad coming with me. That boy has courage and determination."

The kai snorted. "I'm sure you're right. He's like my wife in that regard, I'll wager. However, that same wife will have my balls if I allow his brother to be carted off by a Swarmer captain."

"I will not harm him. I haven't done so, despite not knowing for sure who and what he was. There was perhaps some…humiliation in my tactics," he allowed. "Still, the boy himself is obviously willing to do this."

"It is my duty to protect him, given that I am the only family he has to depend on at the moment."

Sensing an opening, Balto leaned forward, putting his elbows on the table. "You have a duty to your people, too, and under the treaty with Moorcondia for that country as well, I assume."

The kai stiffened. "What of it?"

"What I'm offering you is a kind of treaty, is it not—at least the precursor of one?" When the man nodded in agreement, Balto pressed his argument. "And you are proof that the Chainers and the Moorcondians put a lot of stock in the idea that treaties are stronger when sealed with a formal and personal connection. A marriage, as you call it."

"I don't like where this is headed." The man frowned into his own cup.

"If Cariad is your wife's brother, then he is of a high enough class to bind the treaty. As I've already established, I'm the son of the Swarm's suzerain, and as such, hold sway over the vast network of Swarm-inhabited islands and old factions that still hold tight to their own. A marriage between us would make for a powerful incentive to both of us."

"Do your people even ascribe to the notion of marriage? One hears many things, none of it good. You are entirely hedonistic, I believe."

"You're not wrong. We are looser in our familial ties and don't bind ourselves formally with a lifelong commitment to others the way you do. Some come to it naturally, because it pleases them. Most of us don't know which man actually fathered us, but nevertheless maintain emotional ties to those whom our mothers allow into their homes and beds. It hardly matters, in any event. The concept means something to you and Cariad's king. That's all that counts, and I will take whatever vows you require."

The kai was silent for so long that it seemed he would not respond at all. Then, "You want him." As statements went, it was as blunt as they came.

Balto saw no reason to lie. "I do, yes. How could I not? He's a beautiful boy, with hair the color of the sun and soft skin."

"How do you know what he feels like?"

Balto didn't allow himself to be intimidated by the results of his loose tongue. "I had reason to touch him, now and again. It's a good thing that I am enthralled by him, wouldn't you say?"

Aleki waved off the question. "It doesn't matter what you or I say or think. I won't force Cariad to throw his life away. Once the vows are made and consummated, by Moorcondian law, he will be married to you for the rest of his life. Well, for the rest of *your* life," he added with a menacing grin.

Balto didn't let the implied threat bother him. "My life is precarious, to be sure. I can only promise to do my best to keep the boy safe. And if I fail…" He hated thinking of it, not because his own undoubtedly hideous fate would be the cause of it, but because he knew he was the best hope for his people. "I'll make what arrangements I can to have him spirited away from the citadel and back to you or his own people, whomever my agent finds first."

"I appreciate the sentiment. But if your plot goes to shit, you'll have little power to help him, however much you try. The risk to Cariad's life will be great. Although I hate to send him into danger, I doubt he'll let fear rule his decision. He did volunteer to chart these waters, after all."

"You will give him the choice?" Balto didn't like the idea that he could be thwarted by a mere slip of a boy—and one who'd been mostly hostile toward him...mostly. And it bothered him that he found the boy entirely too appealing for reasons that had nothing to do with his efforts to take control of the Swarm. He'd become accustomed to having him in his cabin and in his bed, even if they did nothing more than sleep. Returning to it without the boy lying next to him was a hard thing to contemplate.

Standing, the kai said, "Of course. He's an adult, so master of his own life, sort of. As much as I'd like to treat him as if he were a child under my control, that simply isn't the case. I will speak to him now. Please make yourself comfortable in my absence."

"I won't try to kill your warriors, if that's what you mean, so long as they don't try to kill me."

They grinned at each other as only two powerful enemies could—part threat and part reassurance. As the kai left the cabin, Balto poured himself more wine and settled in for the wait.

* * * *

Cariad paced the kai's cabin, trying to be patient and keep his annoyance in check. He wasn't going to achieve anything by challenging the man's authority. He had to be cleverer than that and make his case. He wasn't entirely sure he knew what that was, other than a growing certainty that he should return to Balto's ship and sail into the heart of the Swarm's territory with him. Usually when he had to kill time, he spent it drawing. There had been no practical way to bring his writing desk with him, so it remained in Balto's cabin. The knowledge that he'd left something of himself among the man's possessions gave him a strange feeling of contentment.

The door swung open, and the kai entered, not looking happy. The man closed himself in with Cariad, leaving only the two of them and no prying ears. Aleki stood with his hands on his hips and a stern look in his eyes. "I must ask you some questions, and you will give me the truth. I'll tolerate nothing less. Do you understand?"

"Of course. I respect you too much to do otherwise, even if you weren't a member of the Southern Chain's royal family…or my own, for that matter."

The kai gave into a quick smile. "I'm glad you see me as such."

Cariad shrugged. "How else would I view you?"

"Perhaps as the man standing in the way of what you want." Aleki went to sit on the chair of his desk and motioned for Cariad to take the visitor's chair. They sat facing each other, and the kai didn't waste time. "Did Balto touch you?"

Cariad blinked at him a few times as he digested the question. "He didn't rape me, if that's what you mean." Not quite a lie. Even though the blow job would be considered such, he had given it in sacrifice to a cause. Aleki might not see it that way, especially as Balto had admitted he never believed the story of his being a doxy. And there was that strange matter of the man caressing his body in a way that was both sexual and not. Thinking of it raised the hairs on his arms, a reaction that mystified him. He wasn't sure he should have enjoyed it, but it was certainly true that he didn't dislike it. He didn't think that event was what Aleki meant, regardless—or at least he could convince himself of that. Still, he felt comfortable skirting the blurry line of the truth.

Aleki stared at him as if gauging his honesty. "I can see he didn't hurt you, so we'll leave it at that, even though I sense that I'm not getting the entire story." He frowned briefly. "Now, to the present matter. Balto believes strongly that bringing you back to his home will aid in his plan to overthrow his mother. You obviously agree with him."

"I do."

He leaned forward to rest his elbows on his thighs. "It's almost certain death. I don't know anything about the way the Swarm is ruled, but I do know a lot about the history of coups. They are often unsuccessful, and those involved meet terrible fates."

Cariad swallowed down the sudden lump of fear forming in his throat. "I understand. I've read a lot of books on military and political maneuvers myself. I have no illusions about my chances or what might happen to me if Balto fails. It's important that I try, though. Even with the formula for their explosives, it will take our people a long time to mix enough of it and equip our ships with the capability of fighting on their level. I've seen the Swarm ships in action. They are configured very differently than ours."

"I know. My armorer has studied the information Balthazar has given us, and he swears it's genuine, but as you said, scaling it up and finding it useful in battles will be an enormous task."

Now Cariad leaned forward. "Exactly. If Balto succeeds, the war will be over quickly, and we'll be ready if he falters or if he's being duplicitous – which I don't think he is," he hastened to add. "The same skills I employ to draw my charts are easily transferred to producing plans of their citadel's layout. I can honestly say that no one does it better, and we won't have to rely on Balto's skill or honesty if you manage to engage the Swarm on their land."

"You'll get no argument on that point from me. Carwyn has sung your praises, and as you say, such information will prove useful if you find a way to pass them to us, whether Balthazar is successful or not."

"I will do my best, and I'm willing to take the chance that everything will work out by accompanying him to his home."

"Even if it means going secretly as his wife? Which isn't a thing among the Swarm, but I have no other word to describe it. You would be his enslaved whore by their standards. To your king and my prima kailisa, you would go in with a far more important position and bound more tightly to a man who hopefully will be the next suzerain of the Swarm. It will make for a much better outcome to this conflict than we could have ever hoped for. Your service for our cause, however, would never end."

Cariad sat back again, his body going flush all over. *Marry Balto?* It was a frightening thought, although if he were honest with himself, it had crossed his mind already. It was the way of treaties, after all, that it be sealed with such a familial bond. The idea of being tied to the Swarm captain for the rest of his life wasn't entirely unappealing. It meant living away from home, but Carwyn had already taken that step. This wasn't much different, except his brother wanted Aleki, desired him and even loved him. His marriage to Balto would be different. *Won't it?* His sphincter spasmed at the idea of being mounted by the man, so he couldn't claim he didn't desire him. Such physical want was a new experience for him, yet he recognized it for what it was. And protecting his country and family had been his intent from the very start of his journey. This wasn't much different than his volunteering to sail on the Intrepid.

"I understand, of course, kai, and know that my king will not recognize the union if it's not consummated. That step means the union is for life. Having a treaty with the Swarm will always be stronger with my body used as glue."

Aleki looked away, then cleared his throat. "Carwyn told me that you aren't attracted to men."

"I'm not—nor do I have any interest in women." He shrugged. "I've just never understood the need to cater to one's nether regions so assiduously. However…" He struggled to find the right words because he hadn't even really given himself the answer. "Balto is different. I know I should hate him, yet from the moment I set eyes on him, I felt drawn to him. He's so unlike any other man I've ever known. I can't explain it, but I can assure you that I want that particular man. Marrying him won't repulse me, if that's your concern, kai."

"It is. I know how I felt when I was told I had to marry Princess Eleanora. Duty and happiness rarely match up. When the dowager queen hatched her scheme to give me Carwyn instead…? Well, it's hard to describe my feelings when I realized Carwyn stood beside me in that ridiculous shroud they called a wedding gown. It was as if I'd been liberated, and yet I could still do what was best for my people, too. It was a matter of physical attraction. That was before I fell in love with him, mind you. I can't imagine being any happier with my life than I am now. Carwyn feels the same."

"I know." Cariad smiled. "He was very clear on that point." He gnawed at his lower lip. "I can't say that I'll ever feel that sentiment for Balto. I can only assure you that I am willing to serve my people in this way, and I expect to be pleased with my marriage bed." He shrugged. "Does anyone born to the ruling class have the right to hope for anything more? We live to serve as the price for our power." He paused. "Have I convinced you?"

Aleki huffed. "I suppose you have, not that either of us have the luxury of putting your wants ahead of what's best for our people. I believe Captain Balthazar speaks the truth about his quest, and the details he's revealed seem credible and useful, even if he's not successful. It will give us an advantage in this war. Your safety and happiness pale in comparison to what is at stake. And yet..."

Cariad grinned. "And yet, you want to be able to look my brother in the eye and tell him at least I went to my doom as happily as I could. I understand that."

Aleki returned the smile and with a firm nod stood. "Then it's settled. Come now, and as captain of this ship, I'll bind you to him. You may have my cabin for your wedding night."

Cariad couldn't help showing his surprise. "You mean for him to bed me here?"

"I must be able to attest to the consummation. Are you ready?"

Standing on somewhat shaky legs, Cariad didn't think he could give a full-throated answer. "I think so."

"That will have to be good enough."

* * * *

The ceremony took little time, Aleki speaking words that he must have made up as he went along—a mixture of Moorcondian and Chainer customs. To Cariad's ears, it was all so much buzzing, like insects. He heard the words without processing their meaning and responded affirmatively when it was asked of him. Balto did the same, a hint of amusement in his tone. Aleki had said the Swarm didn't practice this kind of ritual, so it must have seemed rather silly to a hardened warrior. He did his part, though. They both did, and before he even realized what was happening, Cariad was escorted back to the kai's cabin and left alone there. There had been talk about the men hammering out a basic treaty and a marriage contract, Aleki standing in for Cariad's parents. That seemed like something that should have happened before the ceremony, but who was he to say? And it didn't matter to him what Balto agreed to on a personal level. Either the man would be kind to him or not. No piece of paper was likely to influence such a hard and commanding warrior. Cariad was due to inherit a small holding when his mother died, but even that held no interest for him. It was so far away, he doubted he could benefit from its income if he spent the rest of his life with Balto.

Not if. I will, whether we die in the near future or a distant one. It all depended on Balto's success, and as there was nothing to be done about that now, Cariad focused instead on the night to come. He paced as he'd done before, then sat and tried to calm himself. Then he nearly jumped out of his skin at the sudden knock on the door. It wasn't Balto, merely a cabin boy bringing a tray of food. Having little appetite, Cariad only picked at some of it and drank a cup of the sweet wine that came with the meal. The alcohol helped soothe his nerves, and although he was tempted to drink more, he decided against it. A mostly clear head was preferable to being too drunk to remember his own wedding night. Good or bad, he wanted the experience to be something that he could mull over in the future to know whether he really enjoyed being mounted by Balto.

It occurred to him that it would be helpful to them both if he was ready once his...*husband* arrived. So, he stripped down to his skin and neatly folded his clothing on the visitor's chair. Pulling back the covers, he lay down on his back and waited...and waited...then waited some more. The time ticked by slowly—or at least he perceived it as such. He worried he might fall asleep before Balto entered, but that was ridiculous. His nerves were still too keyed-up for that. There was no obvious sign that he was aroused in anticipation over what was to happen. The small, limp thing lying between his legs hadn't stirred, and he'd long ago trained himself to stop trying to deliberately wake it up.

When the door opened once more, it didn't startle him as much, but it did cause a shiver to go down his spine. Balto entered, making the spacious cabin appear smaller with his enormous presence. It was doubtful the man would fit comfortably in Aleki's bed. Big as it was, Balto was bigger and longer. The man grinned widely as his gaze slid down Cariad's body. "You seem to have done one of my jobs for me...*wife*. I rather like saying that word," he added as he approached. "It makes me feel possessive. What about you?"

"Me?" Cariad's voice practically squeaked, and this line of questioning was not what he expected. He hadn't really thought they'd talk at all, just get down to the business of sex.

"Do you like thinking of me as your husband?" Balto put a small pot on the shelf built into the wall beside the bed.

"I...um, guess so. I haven't really thought about it. What's that you have?"

"Cream. It will make it easier for you to take my cock. The first time is destined to be uncomfortable, no matter how much care I use, though." He started to undress. "You are a virgin, are you not?"

Cariad looked away and fixed his gaze on the foot of the bed. "Yes." It was silly to be embarrassed by the truth, especially about something that hadn't bothered him before—yet somehow he was.

Balto returned to the bed, having shed all his clothes with surprising speed. Of course, the man was fully erect, that snake tattoo appearing as if it stared back at Cariad. "Your cheeks are delightfully pink." He laughed when Cariad put his hands to his face. "I'm going to enjoy mounting you very much, I think." The Swarmer sat heavily on the side of the bed and put his hand right on Cariad's groin.

His breath caught and he resisted the urge to slide away from the touch. Instead, he lay there, unmoving, and with his gaze fixed on Balto's eyes. He almost missed it when his body started to respond.

Balto's lips spread wide, and his eyes lit up. "There you are." He clasped Cariad's hard dick, his hand easily encircling it completely and nearly encasing the entire shaft, plus his balls. "It only needed a bit of coaxing, and it pleases me very much to see the effect I have on you. This really isn't going to be as much fun for me if you don't join in."

Cariad stuttered out a breath as the man slowly jerked his cock. "I don't understand why you care. It's not as if I have much to offer other than my ass and my mouth, and you can take those however and whenever you like, whether I'm enjoying it or not. My dick isn't something worthy of your attention."

Balto swiped his thumb over the head of Cariad's cock, making him jerk and gasp. "I beg to differ. I find it a fascinating toy."

Cariad rolled his eyes, hating to be forced to point out the obvious. "It's not very big."

"Big enough."

He had no idea what the man meant by that until he let go to brace his hands on each side of Cariad's hips and leaned down to suck the dick all the way into his mouth. With a loud gasp, Cariad went rigid throughout his whole body. He slammed his eyes shut and gripped the bedding as he tried to absorb the intense pleasure that flashed to every nerve ending. Balto had swallowed the entirety of Cariad's dick and balls. The sensation was like being in a warm bath, except the man's mouth actively enveloped it. The Swarmer slid his tongue up and down and all around Cariad's balls and shaft in a rough caress, while his throat muscles massaged the cock repeatedly.

Balto cupped his ass with his large palms to press him closer. His nose tickled the part of his body that connected to the base of his cock. It was impossible for Cariad to move away from the intense assault, nor could he withhold his orgasm. He came explosively with sufficient force to send him bucking up and opened his mouth in a silent scream. No sound could make it past the tight constriction of his windpipe. Balto stayed with him, never stopping his diligent licking and sucking, keeping them joined. As the climax ebbed, he collapsed, his muscles lax and feeling as if his brains leaked out of his ears. He didn't even have the energy to open his eyes. He simply lay there with a pounding heart and labored breath.

Cariad was vaguely aware when his dick and balls plopped out of Balto's mouth, the still-wet skin feeling cool now that it was no longer cocooned. Then the mattress rippled before those big hands that cupped his ass moved to lift his legs and bend his knees until his feet sat flat on the bed. His mind cleared enough for him to realize that his hole was about to be breached, and it was. A slick, blunt object circled the puckered ring before pressing past it. He instinctively stiffened but his boneless state made it a half-hearted effort. It hardly mattered anyway, because his ass was easily conquered, the channel filling with a thickness far too thin to be Balto's cock. Cariad stuttered out a breath and relaxed as the finger fucked him with slow strokes. With each pass, it rubbed against his prostate, and while he knew academically that it was a spot of pleasure for men, he couldn't have imagined how much so.

He moaned and wiggled in reaction to the gentle and steady invasion. Then when Balto didn't attempt to do more, Cariad relaxed again and floated from the effect of the lovely caress. His cock stirred and hardened once more. He could tell that even with his eyes shut by the way it tingled. And, of course, Balto started playing with it, this time running his fingers up and down the shaft with a light touch, before working it with sure, forceful strokes. The combination of the dick-jerking and the finger-fucking sent Cariad into a rush of another climax—except nothing happened. *Damn it!* Balto had moved his hand to tightly grip the base of Cariad's shaft. The maneuver choked the orgasm in its infancy. Cariad whimpered and arched his back.

Balto chuckled. "Don't be in such a rush, darling boy. We have all night to play."

His husband pulled out his finger, despite Cariad's clenching around it. But it came back soon enough with a second finger joining it. This time, his hole was noticeably stretched to a degree that bordered on the painful. The discomfort didn't last long as the gentle fucking began again, along with the slow jerking of his dick. Balto kept up his efforts for a long time, acting as if this was all he wanted to do and could do it forever. Cariad couldn't help but sink into the mattress and let the amazing sensations claim every part of him. Any time he got too close to coming, somehow Balto always knew and cut it off with a tight grip at the base of the dick. Even that frustration turned into a kind of perverse pleasure. Cariad nearly drifted off until the two fingers turned into three. There again, his hole resisted the discomfort of the escalation for a brief time before that rhythmic claiming of his body continued—in and out, and up and down. It felt as if this was the state of being he was always intended to achieve.

Cariad was so relaxed that he almost missed when the final act began. With his grip still on Cariad's shaft, Balto pulled out his fingers and spread Cariad's legs even farther apart. The man positioned his wide body between them and something far larger than any amount of fingers pressed against Cariad's hole. His mind snapped to attention, and just as he started to go rigid with anticipation of the breach, Balto jerked him quickly to a climax. The release captured his attention and shot pleasure through him just as he registered the pain of his husband's enormous dick invading his ass. The dual sensations had him moaning and thrashing his head. He couldn't help pushing out, trying to expel the cock. Instead of getting rid of it, the effort seemed to help it go in even more.

Cariad panted as he tried to adjust. The bit of pain faded to be replaced with an ache, as if his ass was overstuffed—which it was. Nothing so big was supposed to go into it, and yet it had, and the pressure it put on his prostate was a surprising boon. And with Balto still clasping his fingers around Cariad's cock, it started to swell once more. He moaned and bucked his hips again in encouragement. If he could only experience the distraction of another orgasm, being fucked might not be so uncomfortable. As he lay panting, he concentrated on the sensations playing along his shaft and the jolts of pleasure in his balls. He was so consumed by his own physical reactions that it took a while to realize that Balto wasn't moving anything other than his hand, and his breathing was also labored.

Cariad pried his eyes open and stared into those strange violet ones hovering over him. Balto peered down at him with his lips parted and that broad chest of his heaving. The tattoos spread across it rippled as if alive with each breath. And there was enough of the man showing that Cariad could see how only a part of the snake had entered his body. His husband was expending a great deal of effort not to ravish him. He was giving Cariad a chance to adapt to being mounted. It was…sweet. But it also dragged the experience on longer than he thought he could tolerate. This first time with his Swarmer husband was destined to be a mixed experience, part pleasure and part pain. No amount of waiting was going to change that. He realized it was up to him to make the call.

"Fuck me." He pushed the words past his lips, nearly cringing with his conflicted thoughts. He wasn't sure if he was making the right decision, but the mere fact that he seemed to have the control caused his confidence to swell. He was not going to be one step up from a slave with this man. Cariad had some power in the relationship.

Balto hesitated only for a moment before complying. Even then, his movement was slow and shallow. He undulated his hips with no greater speed than a lazy walk in a garden. Sweat dripped off his face, sliding down his broad shoulders and firm pecs, and he fixed his gaze on Cariad's. So he kept his eyes open to show his husband what he was thinking and feeling, to encourage him to claim him as was his right. This was what Cariad had agreed to when he'd spoken his vows. Not explicitly, but this was a part of marriage, and he couldn't claim to be disappointed in the experience of being mounted. There was still discomfort, even with a small amount of Balto's cock inside him. Cariad bit the inside of his cheek in order to hide it. There would be nothing helpful about making his husband feel guilty. *Is that even possible for this Swarmer?* Yes, he was sure of it. No man would strain himself like this to keep from savaging his wife if he didn't have the capacity to empathize or feel shame.

Everything changed in an instant as another climax ripped through him. Cariad cried out and slammed his eyes shut again as the pleasure washed over him. There was a roar and a splash of something warm shooting into his ass, coating his insides and easing the sting of the impalement. As he lay once more melting into the mattress, he was aware of Balto slowly pulling out. Exhausted and feeling shy now that the deflowering was over, Cariad hid behind his closed eyes. Sleep started to claim him, but he was aware of Balto returning and gently wiping him clean, straightening his limp legs and covering him with a warm blanket. There should be some words, he thought, an acknowledgment of what had happened. He couldn't work up the strength to do anything, however, except slip away.

Chapter Six

Balto ignored the two Chainer warriors that followed him as he returned to Aleki's ready room. He understood the need for security and was in far too wonderful a mood to be bothered by anything. It was a good thing he'd taken the time to pull on his trousers before leaving the cabin, too. Otherwise, his happiness would be on display for all to see. As it was, the soft leather barely held his hard dick in check. Anyone with eyes could see that he was not only well pleased by bedding his new wife but also that he was keen to do it all over again. The warm tightness of the boy's ass had been exquisite, and it had taken all his strength not to plow into him fully and vigorously. *Not that I ever will.* Cariad had taken his cock as best as anyone as small as he could have, but there were limits as to how much could be forced with such an unevenly matched couple.

The boy had been stoic about the experience, and better, he'd taken the pleasure Balto had given him with a satisfying enthusiasm. It boded well for their life together. He had feared that the Moorcondian was one of those people who was indifferent to sex, even hostile to it. But that had proven to not be the case. Cariad might have willed away his interest in sex due to his perception that he was not well-endowed as a man, but the concern was rather adorable and completely misplaced. Any man would treasure having such a lovely cock to play with. It made a delightful mouthful, and he hoped his reaction had helped bolster the boy's confidence. Whatever insecurities he'd held before, Balto was sure he'd done a great deal to dispel them.

He scratched at the door to the kai's ready room and waited until he was told to enter. The Chainer captain was still hard at work, pouring over the information Balto had given him with two of his warriors.

Aleki straightened as Balto entered. "Is something wrong?" His tone was sharp and menacing.

Far from being insulted, Balto was glad his wife had powerful men looking out for his interest. He smiled as he approached. "Not at all. I'm merely following what I believe is the custom in Moorcondia, if not in the Southern Chain." He held up the cloth he'd used to wipe Cariad and himself with.

Aleki stared at it, then narrowed his eyes. "Is that a spot of blood I see?"

Balto shrugged. "My wife is small, and I am large. This first time was always going to be difficult, and some minor abrasion occurred. I can assure you, however, that I gave Cariad a great deal of pleasure to outweigh the pain."

Aleki waved his hand. "I don't want that. It may have been a custom in Moorcondia in its darker days, but I don't need any *proof* that the marriage was consummated. It's disgusting and disrespectful to Cariad," he added with a frown.

Balto shrugged. "As you like." He tucked the cloth in his waistband, thinking he might keep it himself. His people were known to keep bloody trinkets from the bodies of their victims, a practice he abhorred. He wasn't sure this reminder of the first night with his wife fell into that category or one of sentimentality. *Probably somewhere in between.* He would think on it, but not share it with Cariad. The boy didn't need to be exposed to anything that might trigger his fear of him or embarrassment. The boy was far too shy as it was. He intended to work on that problem, because he wanted to share everything with his wife that brought pleasure between them without worrying about delicacy.

"Will you return to your ship now?"

"No. Cariad is sleeping, and I don't want to disturb him. Dawn will be soon enough." With that, he took his leave and went back to the cabin where his wife hopefully continued to rest undisturbed.

He did find the boy right as he'd left him, tucked into bed. In sleep, he looked very young. Many of his mother's warriors thought nothing of forcing themselves on children, a practice that he found detestable, even though he held little power to stop it. He would have the ability to do so once he toppled his mother. But he wouldn't have taken Cariad as his wife, even for the sake of success, if the boy weren't actually a man, simply a young one. Cariad was innocent in many ways, yet not naïve. He was smart enough to make the decision to give himself to what had been his enemy—and might still be in his mind, although Balto hated to think so. He could only try as much as possible to prove his worthiness of trust, if not affection. No, that was too great a thing to expect. Their lives together would be one of convenience that benefited both of their peoples' futures. It would be enough if his bride didn't flinch from his touch.

Feeling surprisingly tired himself, Balto shucked off his trousers and hid the cloth within the folds. Then he slipped into bed beside his wife. The boy stirred and murmured something about fucking again, although whether it was from hope or fear, Balto couldn't tell.

He dared to gather Cariad in his arms and was delighted when he snuggled close instead of fighting the embrace. "Go back to sleep, wife. I will keep you safe." *Even from myself.*

* * * *

Balto watched Cariad as Cariad watched Aleki's ship disappear in the distance. The boy had been quiet and compliant as they'd dressed and left. Balto hadn't missed, though, at how his bride had winced as he sat in the dinghy. He knew the boy had to be sore from their coupling, yet he didn't complain. There was nothing to be done about it, either. The cream he'd used to ease the way was also one used on burns, he knew. With a couple of days' rest, the relatively minor damage caused by his dick would be healed. Until he was sure it had, his cock was going to have to be satisfied with other ways to be pleasured. And there was fun to be had in giving to one's bed partner as well as taking it from them. He could hardly wait to shower his wife with the kind of attention that made him hard and come with sweet, breathy moans. It made him feel quite the accomplished lover, although he'd never worried much about that before. Cariad was different, somehow. He wanted him more than he had others, with a bone-deep intensity that mystified him. *And those thoughts are not helping*. He adjusted his tunic as he joined Cariad at the railing.

"I wish Aleki's men didn't have to make the journey imprisoned in your hold."

"They have to appear as if they've had a rough time of it when I hand them over as tribute to my mother. They understand the need and remember that Aleki had ordered no one. They are all volunteers. And I promise they will be dirty and smelly when they are taken off this ship, but no harm will come to them. My crew understand they are not to abuse them."

"I know." He sighed. "They are very brave to volunteer to do this."

"No more than you are," Balto couldn't help pointing out. His wife seemed intent on downplaying his own worthiness.

"It doesn't take courage to have your dick sucked. Does your ship have a name?" The sudden change in topic surprised Balto. Before he could answer, his wife clarified. "I ask because I was on the Intrepid. All Moorcondian ships are given a name, usually one picked by whoever the queen is at the time. Chainers give theirs numbers. Aleki's is 'ship number one' and so on, which I'm sure you've already noticed from his flag. My brother, Carwyn, told me they think it's odd that we treat our ships almost like people." He cocked his head to look at Balto. "What do you do?"

Balto grimaced, knowing that the answer wasn't going to be one that his wife would like. "We name it after its captain, so it changes. Mine is called 'Bloodletter'. Remember that I'm known among my people as 'Balthazar the Bloodletter'," he clarified, because his wife needed to keep in mind everything about them if they were to make a successful life together.

"Have you killed so many people, then?" he asked in a soft voice. "You said your grandfather and mother raised you to want to do it."

Balto placed his finger under the boy's chin so that they could look each other in the eye. It was gratifying when his wife didn't flinch. "I have, yes, because, as you remarked, I was raised to and did so before I had even been bedded for the first time. I went out on Malachi's ship when he was made a new captain. He led a raid on a ship of what I could see to be pirates, so it didn't really bother me to kill such men, because they were also murderers. All that blood and gore up close sickened me, although I was careful not to show it. And my brother celebrated my *accomplishment* once we returned to the citadel by taking me to a brothel. He handed me over to the most beautiful woman I'd ever seen, the madam of the house actually, so she was quite a bit older than I was—not that it diminished her desirability to most men. She was smart as well, because she understood once we were alone that she held no interest for me. My clumsy efforts didn't give me away, but my cock remained limp, even as I held her ample breasts. When she sneaked in a man… Well, it was an experience that helped cleanse my mind of the horror of what I'd done. And I've stuck with men since then, although they have typically been other warriors. I don't like to take advantage of slaves or others who may not have much of a choice in being with me."

"Please don't put me in that category. I'm right where I want to be." A ghost of a smile crossed Cariad's face. "My brother took me to a brothel, too, not in celebration of anything. He was peeved for some reason that I didn't seem to be interested in sex. He couldn't fathom why, and I had no words to explain it, either. It was really none of his business, anyway, but older brothers think they know everything, so…I didn't want the pretty girl who took me by the hand, nor was I interested in a boy when she offered." He shrugged. "We spent the time talking about flowers. She was a keen horticulturist on her off hours. Then she praised my prowess when she returned me to my brother. It was kind of her—and it seemed to satisfy my brother's worries."

Balto rubbed his thumb along his wife's soft jaw. "I can't change my past, but please understand that what I'm intent on doing started with my holding my sword in check and capturing instead of killing. Slavery is horrible, but at least it's life. Death kills hope, along with the body." Balto moved his hand to slide his thumb across his wife's plump lips. It occurred to him that he hadn't kissed them yet. A boy like Cariad would want such tenderness. "I don't want you to be afraid of me. I know I hurt you last night."

Cariad surprised him by gripping the hand that touched him. "No more than was necessary. I could tell how careful you were being. It must have been…difficult to hold back like that."

"You are more than worth the effort, wife." Balto gave into the impulse to do that thing he'd rarely done with anyone. He leaned down and pressed his mouth against Cariad's, nibbling at it softly before taking it more eagerly. Cariad didn't pull away, encouraging him to do more. He ran his tongue against the seam of the boy's lips in a gentle demand to be let in. The mouth was warm and sweet-tasting. Far from being passive, Cariad moaned into him and shyly twined his tongue with Balto's. It was only the need to breathe that caused him to break the kiss. Cariad looked at him with a slightly dazed expression.

Balto was well pleased with his efforts. "Come… We should eat breakfast."

Somehow, they ended up holding hands as they walked to his cabin. Tasha had already delivered a tray of food and drink. She and the cook always managed to conjure up fresh, delicious meals. His stomach tightened with hunger, reminding him that Cariad was probably even more hungry.

"Go sit at my desk and begin eating." He no sooner than ushered his wife over to the seat than Pia crawled through the open window and leaped onto his shoulder. "Ah, miss me, did you?" He chucked her under her chin before snagging a piece of fruit and handing it over to her.

She cupped it in her human-like paws and devoured it with the same enthusiasm as Cariad was showing toward his piece of buttered bread and a thick slice of cheese. When Balto got some food of his own, the monkey surprised him by leaving him to sit on the desk next to Cariad. She chittered away as she took another piece of fruit for herself.

Cariad froze. "Is she angry with me?"

Balto chuckled, an unexpected warmth spreading through him at the sight. "Quite the contrary. This is her way of showing that she likes you. Monkeys are smart creatures. I bet she senses that we are now intimate, which makes you part of her family. Be forewarned, darling boy, that the next move may be…that," he finished as Pia crawled up to squat on Cariad's shoulders.

"Oh!" Despite his obvious discomfort, the boy picked up a piece of fruit and handed it to Pia. He giggled when she took it from him and started eating. "She's sweet, isn't she? It's a little unnerving, though, how much they are like us."

"She is and it is, but I found her on an island in the arms of her dead mother, and for some reason, I just couldn't leave her there."

"You have compassion," Cariad said as if it were a simple and obvious fact.

No one had ever said such a thing to him before. It startled him how much he appreciated hearing it, yet wasn't sure what to say in response. Clearing his throat, he changed the topic. "I must go up on deck and check in with my men. Will you be all right on your own down here?"

Cariad raised his eyebrows. "I've spent a lot of time in this cabin already, remember? I'll be fine, although I do want to go up there later in the day. I need to watch for islands and document their location. I will also need to spend time looking at the night sky for better bearings."

"You are not a prisoner, darling boy. Not anymore," he amended. "You may go where you like, including coming with me."

He gave him a pretty smile. "Thanks, but the sun is too bright. I have to wait until it's past its zenith or my skin burns." Giving Balto a curious look, he asked, "Do you Swarmers use a protective cream or something? You're even paler than I am. Why aren't you bothered by the sun?"

Balto swallowed his last bite of food. "I have no idea. Our skin is indifferent to the heat and brightness. It's never occurred to me that anyone else's isn't. The

Chainers and other indigenous people don't seem affected by it, either—or not by much. We should keep that vulnerability of the Moorcondians secret. My mother will use any perceived weakness against her enemies."

"I understand and agree. We have a lot to learn about each other, it seems. I suppose we'll have many days to do so before we reach the citadel."

"Yes, many days yet." And because he wanted to kiss the boy again, then carry him into bed, Balto backed away and left the cabin without so much as a backward glance.

* * * *

Amadeus leaned against the wall, watching Balto steer as there was nothing in particular for him as second in command to do at the moment. The crew knew their tasks and needed little oversight, and Balto didn't mind the company. "So, what is the marriage thing all about?"

Balto didn't bother to even give the man a sideways glance. His attention was taken by the sight of his wife sitting cross-legged on the hatch with his drawing desk across his lap. "It's about promising to spend the remainder of one's life with another. I didn't pay much attention to what was said by the Chainer captain or what he expected me to say in return. All that mattered was that Cariad said the words, and they had meaning for him."

"Our people do form families in a similar way sometimes. More so, I believe, before your grandfather unified us all and demanded fealty to him alone. I've never heard of a ceremony being done, though."

"The old bastard wanted to discourage even personal alliances in favor of devotion to him, that is true. He would have eradicated any customs that worked against that goal. My mother sees the wisdom in keeping with that strategy, although I don't think she really cares—so long as her God of Blood gets his due."

"If the wind keeps up at this strength, we'll be back home in time for the full moon. The captain from the Intrepid will meet his fate on her altar."

"I am aware." There was a bite to his tone that he hadn't intended. He'd already considered the timing.

"We could slow down."

"No. Our plan doesn't benefit from us doing so. The greater good must trump my wife's feelings. Seeing his old captain die like that will be very hard on him for certain. I will do my best to shield him from the worst of it."

"I'm sure you will." Amadeus was quiet for a while. "How is it between you and the boy? He seems comfortable around you, when I would have expected him to be… I don't know."

Balto spared him a glance. "Fearful? Resigned to a fate worse than death being tied to a big brute such as myself?"

"I meant no disrespect. It's simply that he is a small man—almost delicate, I'd say—and probably untried in being bedded, notwithstanding his ridiculous claim of being a whore."

"Are you looking for a description of how I spent the wedding night with my bride?" He kept his tone light, not being offended by the turn their conversation had taken. Amadeus was his closest friend, and he'd shared everything with him since childhood. Without his support, Balto's half-formed idea of overthrowing his mother might never have become a reality.

Amadeus snorted. "I don't need to hear anything about it to know that you are well pleased. And the boy's demeanor indicates that he wasn't unmoved by the experience, even if his movements are gingerly. I was surprised to see that the Moorcondians are even smaller than the Chainers. Perhaps we of the Swarm are the largest humans to roam the world."

"I believe my wife is not representative of his people. He's probably on the shorter side and more slender, based on what we've seen so far of their sailors and the few facts about Moorcondians warriors Aleki gave me. And what you say about us may be true, but regardless, I was careful with my wife, frustratingly so. I don't like causing him pain, and that would be true even if I hadn't promised not to do so in the marriage contract."

"What is that?"

"It's like a treaty between families. Kai Aleki stood in for Cariad's family. Among other things, I had to swear I would never beat him."

Amadeus barked out a laugh. "If they worried you'd do so, why would they ever give him to you?"

"Needs must," was the simple answer. "We're all doing what's best for the future of our peoples. It was their version of our blood sacrifice. I could tell the man was conflicted, but Cariad didn't appear to be. He is a pleasure in bed, as it happens. And apparently upon his mother's death, he will own a profitable holding, whatever that means. I have promised to leave it in his hands. Not that I care… I would never take his wealth for my own purposes, but apparently the Moorcondians worry about such matters."

"They treat it like a business transaction, as if you are bartering in a marketplace."

"That was my take, as well." At that moment, his wife turned his head and looked at him. He smiled and gave a little wave before returning to his work. The brief interaction made Balto ridiculously happy.

"I can see how he might prove passionate and enjoy being in your bed, despite his ignorance of it all," Amadeus mused. "I've seen the looks in the eyes of slaves who must warm their masters' or mistress' beds. There is a fear and anger there that can't quite be hidden. It's why I use brothels, even though my new house slave strikes my fancy. I don't want to force her and worry that the interest I think I see lurking in her eyes is no more than her desire to not anger me. So long as she's a slave, I can never be sure if she is willing, even if I say I am giving her a choice."

"When we are victorious, you'll be able to free her and know one way or another." He'd almost said 'if' but he couldn't think like that. He had to go into this certain of triumphing.

"I hope you're right. I see nothing like what I worry about in your wife's expression."

"Neither do I, but it's good to have confirmation of it from you."

"Does he not know we have charts of these waters?"

"He does, yes, but needs to see for himself. There is something about how his mind works, his perception of the world, that requires him to actively study his surroundings, then he's able to commit the images to memory."

"I'm not sure how that helps our cause."

"Neither do I. Our new allies have the knowledge I gave them to find the citadel. But as they probably don't trust us all that much, it gives them comfort to know Cariad is keeping track himself." What he didn't say was how he hoped the activity occupied his wife's attention to distract him from what lay ahead. The central city of the Swarm was a dark and nasty place. It would dampen the light that was Cariad with shocking ease. He knew the boy would hate it and could only hope that he could shield him from the worst of it.

* * * *

Cariad rolled over onto his side to face Balto. They'd been lying side-by-side in his huge bed after a surprisingly low-keyed exchange of blow jobs. He'd come immediately, of course, when Balto had sucked him into his mouth, having no control over himself. He hoped that would change, because he really did want to make the experience last. His own efforts to please his husband had been better than his first disastrous try, but he was never going to be able to swallow the man's cock the way he did with his. It was enough that he'd taken more than before and hadn't dribbled as much cum. His husband did release more than a mouthful of the stuff. And perversely, he was a little disappointed that it hadn't shot into his ass like it had the night before. He understood why Balto had killed that idea when Cariad had raised it. He was still sore, and the sting that came from washing himself told him that no amount of prepping had made him supple enough to accept the man's dick without abrading his tender skin.

He felt unfulfilled, however, and wasn't ready to go to sleep. Reaching out his hand tentatively, he asked, "May I touch you?"

Balto slanted his heavy-lidded eyes in his direction. "Please yourself, wife."

Cariad placed his palm lightly on the closest pec. "You like calling me that, don't you?"

"As it happens, I do." He grimaced. "I'm sorry that I'm going to have to use insulting names once we reach my home."

Cariad caressed an ornate and colorful representation of some flora that he didn't recognize splashed across his husband's chest. "I understand. There, everyone expects me to be your slave." He curled his fingertips as a thought crossed his mind. "You'll have to tattoo me, won't you?"

Balto covered his hand with his own and surprised Cariad by raising it to his lips. He kissed the backs of the fingers before returning the hand to his chest. "I won't mark you with a permanent tattoo. It will be like Tasha's—drawn with a durable ink that eventually washes off."

Cariad slid his palm down his husband's abdomen, enjoying the way the prominent muscles rippled under this touch. "I thought Tasha was your slave, really and truly."

"She is, but only to protect her. Her father has been my mother's slave since he was captured in a raid before I was born. When Tasha was of an age to be branded as a slave and perhaps sold off, I asked for her as a way of keeping her safe. My mother made me pay a pretty price, but the cost meant nothing to me. I didn't have the heart to mar Tasha's lovely face, however, so I keep her onboard ship with me in order to make sure no one accidently notices how the mark fades and has to be reapplied."

"For someone called the Bloodletter, you are awfully kind." Cariad dared to keep going and clasp Balto's hardening cock. He couldn't quite close his fist all the way around it. *No wonder it hurt when this thing entered my body. Will there come a time when I will be able to take all of it?* He rubbed his thumb across the snake's beady eyes. "This is the real thing, though, isn't it? I mean a tattoo, ink etched into your skin and not the kind that washes off."

"Yes." His husband sounded slightly winded.

"It must have been horribly painful."

"It was, indeed. And as my brother was watching me the whole time because we've been goaded into constant competition since we were young boys, I had to pretend it didn't. Any sign of weakness is a thing to be exploited, you see."

"You are very brave." He squeezed the shaft, enjoying the feel of the velvety skin.

Balto closed his eyes on a low groan. "Not really. Much of what I've done in life was born of fear. I've had enough of that for myself and most everyone else in my mother's control. I want to liberate us all from that terror." He gave no warning other than a stuttering breath before his dick swelled within Cariad's grasp and unloaded copious amounts of his seed over Cariad's fingers and his own groin.

"Was that all right?" Cariad asked in a low voice, pleased with his efforts, while also uncertain of what liberties he could take.

"You never have to ask if making me climax is acceptable. Take it on faith, wife, that I enjoy your attention."

Cariad smiled, smugly, he was sure. This was a new and exciting experience for him, and he was glad to learn that sex with the right person for him was as enticing as it seemed to be for everyone else. He wasn't so different after all, only needed to meet someone who could awaken his sexuality. When he went to leave the bed to wash his hand, Balto held him in place.

Then he wiped the cum off with a corner of the blanket before tossing it over them both. "We'll no doubt dirty the bedding up more before the night is done, so there's no need to inconvenience yourself. Tasha will do the laundry tomorrow."

Cariad snuggled into the man's side, liking the warmth against his skin. "How embarrassing."

"I am of the opinion, wife, you sometimes think too much. Everyone onboard ship knows we have sex, and there are likely many of them similarly engaged with each other. Go to sleep now. We will be sailing many days before we arrive home."

Home. He wondered if he would ever come to think of the citadel of the Swarm as such. As long as Balto was there and in control, he thought maybe he could.

Chapter Seven

Cariad stood by the railing to see as much of the citadel as he could while the Bloodletter sailed into port. It sat at near the top of a rocky island with sparse vegetation, a city sprawled out in rings down to the sea, with the castle towering over it all and surrounded by a high stone wall. It was all foreboding, a place no one would choose to live in—or, at least, he couldn't imagine wanting to do so if his circumstances were different. What he could imagine was the leader of the Swarm—the suzerain as Balto referred to her—standing at the highest tower of her lair, looking down on all the rest. It was certainly a defensible position, and if they had dug deep wells within, they would have an unlimited supply of water while under siege. Undoubtedly they'd stored stolen grain and dried goods to last a long time, as well. Whether the enemy came from the outside or from among her own people, Balto's mother wouldn't be easy to unseat. While Balto hadn't told him much about his plot for Cariad's own safety, they had to include attacking first from within.

The fake tattoo that had been inked on his face the day before itched. He had to stop himself numerous times from scratching it. If anyone noticed it wasn't permanent, it would give away too much of what was going on inside Balto's head. Cariad wanted to help his husband and both their peoples as best he could, and that meant acting like a brutalized slave. That didn't mean he had to hide away, but as he mapped out what he saw in his mind, he tried to appear submissive to any eyes that bothered to look at him. His hair whipped annoyingly around his face, but Balto had said it needed to stay down. It was the thing that marked him in particular as worthy of being the bed-warmer of the Bloodletter—the man, not the ship. *How confusing.* As they neared the dock, the bothersome strands paled in comparison to the sudden fear that laced his guts. Every member of the Swarm within sight of their approach seemed to be making their way down to greet their ruler's son.

Balto surprised him by coming to him suddenly. "Amadeus has taken the wheel, and I'm sorry for this." It was all the warning he gave before buckling a leashed leather collar around Cariad's neck. Then he yanked him down to his knees.

Even knowing that it was all done as a show for those who watched them, Cariad's heart tripped into a rapid beat of fear. He wanted to look into his husband's eyes to gain some comfort there, but he knew that wasn't the right thing to do. So he kept his gaze downward and didn't move a muscle until the ship lurched against the dock and Balto tugged him back to his feet.

As they headed to the gangplank, Aleki's warriors were dragged onto the deck with hands tied behind their backs and tied to each other by a rope around their necks. They .were dirty and disheveled, just as Balto had intended. They shot murderous looks at the Swarm while keeping their heads high. Even knowing they were volunteers who played a role as beaten-down prisoners, it made him sick to his stomach to see it.

Balto gave him no opportunity to dwell on the warriors further. He walked down to the docks, keeping Cariad literally on a short leash. The crowd was quiet until he took his first step onto the dock. Then as they parted with bowed heads to give him room to pass, they started chanting. "Bloodletter. Bloodletter." Their voices were low at first, then got stronger and louder until they were shouting it as he and Balto reached a huge, black horse. The creature snorted at his arrival and tossed its head. The man holding a rope hung around the horse's neck bowed low. Strangely, there was no saddle.

Cariad had to bite back a squeal as Balto grabbed him by the waist and slung him over the back of the horse. Cariad's head swam at being upside down. Then Balto vaulted up behind his hanging body and pressed one hand on the small of his back to steady him. It was a horribly uncomfortable position, and he was glad his nerves had kept him from eating more than a token amount that morning. He very much feared he would lose the contents of his stomach soon. When Balto kicked the horse into a walk, Cariad realized that his husband had both hands on him now. He must have removed the rope and was keeping his mount under control with his legs alone. It would have been an impressive feat if Cariad weren't so dizzy and nauseated.

The ride up to the castle was long. To keep himself from panicking, Cariad focused on what he could see. The road was mostly packed dirt with some rough stones embedded in it to keep it from running completely downhill when it rained. The people of the Swarm stood on either side of it, watching them make their slow assent. Most of them were like Balto and his crew—tall and pale with black hair. There were others, though. Chainers and people like them from the sacked islands weaved among the crowd, unquestionably slaves and going about their duties to avoid punishment. A few he spotted had dark skin and curly hair like Tasha. No one he saw looked like him. He was undoubtedly a great prize, being a Moorcondian. He wondered where the other survivors from the Intrepid were. He remembered Balto's brother saying something about sacrificing Captain Ambrose. Because his already queasy stomach lurched at the thought, he put it aside and concentrated on mapping his way up to the castle.

When they passed the gates of the structure's protective wall, he knew they were almost at their destination. Balto stopped the horse without warning, vaulted off it and slid Cariad to his feet. He swayed as his head swam once more from the abrupt change. It was bad enough to struggle to get his land-legs back. This short journey slung over the back of a horse had left him disoriented. But it hardly mattered anyway. Balto pushed him down to his knees once more. Cariad winced at the impact, tried to catch his breath and hold down his breakfast. Using the leash, Balto tugged him against his leg. Cariad gratefully leaned into his strength and could feel the change in him the moment it happened. There was a stiffening, and he tightened his grip on the leash enough to cause the collar to bite into Cariad's neck. He couldn't hold back the whimper, which was probably a good thing for those watching and studying them. Balto loosened his hold immediately, however.

Brisk footsteps approached them until Cariad could see black boots and black leather trousers, even with his gaze cast downward. There was a whip coiled in a hand that was clearly a woman's. It wasn't small or delicate, exactly, but more so than Balto's or those of the man standing beside her.

"Welcome home, Bloodletter." The female voice held a surprisingly sensuous tone with a hint of malice that caused a shiver to run down Cariad's back.

"I am honored by your personal greeting, Eminence."

There was a throaty bit of laughter before the woman came closer. "No need for formality, my dear son." Leaning in, she gave Balto some sort of embrace.

Something made Cariad glance up at that moment. That's why he caught the brief look of hatred on the brother's face—Malachi. The man replaced it with a feral grin. "Yes, it is good to see you again, Balto. I see that you were successful in your hunt." It pissed the guy off. That was obvious.

"Yes, I found a Chainer ship. Unfortunately, I was only able to capture a few warriors for the slave auction. The rest fought to the death. One can't help but admire their choice."

"Not like the Moorcondians, heh?" his brother sneered. "They fetched a pretty price for her eminence's coffers, though. And I see that you've still got their captain's slut."

"Observant as always, Malachi." Balto's tone was no less dismissive.

"I've found mine to be deliciously tight and easily broken in as a dutiful slave, although slow and clumsy. Sometimes I think he likes doing something that earns him a beating."

Thinking of the cabin boy, Sean, Cariad had a hard time keeping his emotions in check and showing nothing in his expression.

Balto threaded his fingers through Cariad's hair and forced his face up. "They're just dumb, frightened creatures, brother. It takes patience to train them properly. See how docile mine is?"

Before Malachi could respond, the suzerain laughed again. "Oh, you boys, always competing. It keeps me guessing as to who will succeed me." The woman was nearly as tall as her sons and was indeed dressed very much like them as well. Her hair was far longer, however, and her tunic fell to the tops of her thigh-high boots in the front, and almost to her ankles in the back. It flared out when she abruptly turned around to mount the steps of the castle.

Malachi bared his teeth at Balto before following her. Cariad was forced to his feet by Balto's grip on his hair. He was grateful for the hold, truth be told, as his knees went weak as he climbed the steps to enter the dark maw of the gray stone building. He wasn't so scared that he didn't remember to gaze about to memorize his surroundings. It was immediately apparent to him that the inside didn't look as big as the outside, a difference that couldn't be explained by the thickness of the walls alone. *There are rooms within rooms and probably secret passageways to access them.* It was obvious to him, but did others see it or know about it?

Probably not. Moorcondians had often employed such architecture for either the convenience of servants or for worried hosts to spy on their guests. It was easily unnoticed…unless one had a mind like Cariad's. He was concentrating on the configuration of each room he passed through and the stairs that he climbed. He didn't notice they had arrived at Balto's suite of rooms until the man kicked the big, wooden door shut behind them.

His husband let go of him immediately and unhooked the leash. Then he whirled Cariad around and took him by the shoulders. "Are you all right? The journey slung over my horse was awful, I know."

Cariad felt his cheeks warm at Balto's intense gaze, and his fright took a step back as arousal rose. "It wasn't so bad. I do wish you had warned me about it."

Balto cupped his face. "I thought of telling you many things, but too much knowledge will either scare you more than I would like or cause you to show less fear than others must see." He surprised Cariad with a soft kiss that morphed into a more passionate one. This was not something they did a lot, but Cariad loved it and wanted to find a way to encourage the gesture of affection without demanding more of this husband than the man could give. The sweet interlude was interrupted by the door opening again.

A man, dark like Tasha, but also a dwarf, came strolling in as if it were his chambers. He had a closely cropped and curly beard over his lower face that almost obscured his slave's tattoo. Even so, Cariad could see that it was a little different than his own. "So you come home once more with bounty, heh, boy?"

Wrapping his arm around Cariad's waist, he held him fast to his side. "It was a very fruitful time at sea,

Pele. And as you can see, I found something quite rare and fetching."

"I look forward to hearing all about it—later, when we have a quiet moment together." He tugged at his ear and shook his head.

"Perhaps after the ceremony. For now, you can fetch me a mug of wine. And bring one for my slut. I find him more…pliable when he has alcohol in him. But add some of those herbs you carry, as his stomach is undoubtedly uneasy. I don't want him throwing up on me." He went to sit on a stuffed chair by a low fire. Cariad knelt beside him without being told to.

The slave, Pele, brought them both some wine and winked when he handed Cariad his mug. "This will put you right. I must go to my mistress now and help her prepare," the man added for Balto's benefit. "I just wanted to welcome you." With that, the man bowed and left the room.

Cariad sipped his wine and looked around what was a sitting room with an archway through which he could just make out a bed. Everything was a strange mixture of plain military usefulness with luxurious embellishment. He had a million questions to ask his husband but didn't dare voice them. His interpretation of Pele's words and actions was that people might be listening to them, perhaps even watching them. At least some in the household, including Balto, knew about the possible passageways. He saw no obvious place where that could be done, but he figured he could reason out any hidey-holes if he were able to look.

"Your pardon, master. May I walk around to regain my land legs?"

With a wave, Balto said, "Do as you like, so long as you keep your ass handy."

Cariad rose slowly, being truly unsteady on his legs, and made a slow circuit of the room. Through parted curtains, he peered out of the windows, gauging the gap between the outer walls and those of the chambers. There was nothing obviously off about the configuration, so he kept looking. The bedchamber was much like any other he'd ever seen, except for the size of the bed. Four Moorcondian soldiers could sleep in it quite comfortably. He hoped to be able to lie there instead of on the floor while Balto slept. His husband had to keep up the appearance that he was a slave and Balto was the Bloodletter. That meant not coddling him at a minimum and likely delivering an occasional slap in case anyone watched.

He tried to appear meek and merely curious as he walked around this inner room, and here he could see that it was too small and the walls thicker than they needed to be. A privy and bathing chamber was attached to the far end. It looked harmless enough, but he bet there were smaller holes among the larger ones that someone could use to listen in on private conversations. He wondered whether he and his husband were ever going to be able to talk freely. And how had the man managed to collect a coterie of like-minded people to plot to overthrow the suzerain? He supposed he would find out soon.

A troop of slaves, as well as servants, met him on his way back to Balto. They carried buckets of steaming water to fill the tub he'd seen. When he entered the sitting room, more were setting up a small amount of food on a table. Balto rose lazily, and draining his mug, he tossed it to someone who caught it with admirable agility. The man slowly stripped off his clothes, dropping them on the floor as he went. Onboard ship, he'd been neat and tidy. Here he acted like a man who knew others were there to clean up his mess. Even knowing it was a façade, Cariad had a hard time watching his husband treat the servants and slaves alike as if they existed solely for his benefit. The difficulty only ratcheted up when Balto grabbed him by the hair as he passed on his way to the bathing chamber.

His husband only let him go when he stepped into the now-filled tub. He flicked his gaze at him. "Strip off your clothes or they will get wet when you wash me." He shook his head. "Your stupidity continues to surprise me. Fortunately for you, your ass is tight."

Cariad didn't have to pretend to be hurt by the man's words. As he removed his clothing and folded them on the floor with care, he kept his back turned and let his anger and misery show on his face. If anyone was watching them, they would have no doubt that he wasn't happy with his treatment. And it should have been a fun chore to soap his husband's body up with the fragrant spicy soap he found in a nearby pot. Instead, his hands shook a bit as he sat on the edge of the tub.

Balto lay dispassionately while Cariad ran a soapy cloth along his shoulders and chest. He had to struggle to hold the man's arms up, especially the one on the far side. His husband made no effort to help him and naturally all that touching had the obvious effect. Cariad didn't have to be told to reach into the water and jerk the man off.

* * * *

There were many important matters that should be plaguing his mind, yet Balto could only think of how unfair it was that his first bath shared with his wife had to be such a miserable one—for both of them. Cariad wasn't feigning his anger over his treatment. Even understanding the why of it, as he was sure the boy did, wasn't enough for his tender feelings to let Balto's harshness slide off his back. He'd wanted nothing more than to gather his wife in his arms and soothe away the hurt, but to do so would be madness. The walls had eyes and ears, he was sure of it, even though he had no idea how or exactly where. Pele had been the one to warn him of the passageways, and Balto had worried himself over whether he should tell Cariad before they'd landed. Fearing that the boy would give away too much by his actions, he'd kept it to himself, as he had so many other things. But when his wife had roamed through his suite, he'd known he'd figure it out for himself.

It still didn't thaw the chill between them.

He tossed a piece of bread at the boy as he sat at his feet. "Eat. You'll get little more at the banquet unless I'm feeling charitable, which as you've learned I rarely am."

"Thank you, master." Cariad's voice was quiet and submissive.

Balto ate sparingly himself as the banquet would be soon and the ceremony after it would be too stomach-turning to fill up with food. He would have to find a way to spare his wife the worst of it. There was no chance to keep the boy here instead of dragging him along. Mal would certainly bring one of his slaves, as the bloody sacrifice aroused him. The fucker actually enjoyed having his cock sucked as he watched their mother plunge her knife into the victim. Still, as revolting as the notion was, it might serve a purpose.

At least the poor slave stuffed with Mal's dick couldn't see the barbarous act.

And as if his thoughts could conjure the asshole, his door swung open and in swaggered his older brother, the cabin boy from the Intrepid trailing by a leash. The poor lad sported a bruised cheek and walked as if he were in pain, which undoubtedly he was. Mal wouldn't have taken any care in mounting the boy, and like their mother, he enjoyed whipping his slaves.

"Ah, Balto, enjoying fresh land food I see."

Balto kicked back his legs and slumped into his chair. "I do enjoy my time at sea, but being home is a rare treat, for both of us I'll wager. Please join me."

His brother sat in the empty chair, tossing his slave to the floor next to Cariad. The two boys shared a commiserating look before keeping their gazes down. Balto lazily dropped his hand on the top of his wife's head. He toyed with the hair as if amusing himself when what he really hoped he was doing was soothing Cariad. The boy had shown remarkable restraint and flexibility, even though he must be frightened half out of his mind. It was frustrating to be unable to show him any amount of reassurance or…affection. Yes, that's what he felt compelled to do. The Moorcondian was not simply a means to an end or an enticing place in which to stick his cock. He liked Cariad, and that put the boy in a very select group of people.

"Looking forward to the ceremony?" Mal shot him a baiting grin, knowing there was only one acceptable answer and sensing, as always, that Balto hated it all.

He affected a nonchalance. "Of course. To feel otherwise would be disrespectful to Lilith."

"You choose your words carefully, Balto. If you weren't such a fierce warrior, you'd make a fine courtier. Not that you've done much killing of late." He drank deeply from his cup, his eyes on Balto.

"Slaves captured for selling are more profitable than anything we seize from our raids. I can satisfy my bloodlust with fewer kills."

"Hmm. Your cut from the Chainer warriors will be substantial, I must admit. They will be invaluable in the quarries." He flicked his gaze at Cariad. "That pretty piece would fetch a goodly sum, as well. He looks as exciting as a bowl of gruel, though. Surely you are tired of him at this point."

Because he could see the cruel desire in his brother's eyes, Balto shut that topic down quickly. "The slut is tight and biddable. I'm still well pleased."

Mal pushed over his own slave with the toe of his boot. The boy landed with a thud and a whimper. "This one bores me. He was more entertaining when he fought me, but my dick broke him too quickly."

Because Cariad practically vibrated with anger beneath his touch, Balto tightened his grip on the hair and tugged. "You've always been impatient, Mal. Savoring the journey is at least as fun as arriving at your destination." He used his hold to drag Cariad closer and pushed his face onto his thigh. It gave him the opportunity to gentle his touch and soothe as best he could where Mal couldn't see. It was hard not to smile when the boy wrapped his arms around his leg and held on tightly.

Mal sighed. "I suppose that means you're not interested in a trade."

"No, but I might buy yours off you—at a discounted price, naturally, seeing as how you've broken him in a little too well. It might be amusing to watch the two sluts fuck each other." He licked his lips obscenely, knowing his brother's views all too well.

Mal stared at him with a look that Balto knew meant that his brother was scheming in some way. "How about a different kind of trade? It has occurred to me that it could be good sport to turn one of those Chainer warriors into a slut. Such a man would find the experience unbearable humiliating, and I'd find it more of a challenge to break one. What do you say?" he asked before draining his cup.

There was a calculation in the offer, more than the obvious one that Mal really would enjoy debasing a proud and strong man. Balto just couldn't see what it was. "Hardly an even transaction, and you know I'm not generous of spirit, even for my dear brother."

Mal got to his feet. "I can sweeten the deal for you. I'm sure we'll come to some kind of arrangement. We'll speak of it more later. See you at dinner." Snapping his fingers at his slave, he strode to the door, tugging the leash as he went. The boy scrambled to follow him before choking.

When they were alone again, Balto skimmed his thumb across Cariad's exposed cheek, hoping to provide comfort while not showing overt compassion in case any prying eyes watched. "You'd like it if I acquired your friend, wouldn't you?" He asked the question in a low voice, trying to plaster a lascivious grin on his face.

Cariad gave him a pleading look. "Yes, master."

"I shall consider it, but you'll have to show me more gratitude than usual."

"Yes, master." Then Cariad closed his eyes. A teardrop trickled down his cheek.

Wishing he could do more, Balto petted his wife and plotted his next moves. The rebellion had to wait until the Chainer and Moorcondian ships had time to surround the outer waters of the citadel. It put his plans back by a significant amount of time yet increased the chances of success tremendously. It didn't mean, though, that he shouldn't or couldn't put the first line of attack in place. Everything would be ready to begin at his command. And he needed to keep a better eye on Malachi. Their mother lived in her own world of blood and madness. Her older son, however, had his own agenda. He was planning something himself. Balto was sure of it. The question was...what?

Chapter Eight

The night sky was clear, allowing the full moon to shine brightly down on the sacrificial altar, and the air was still. It was the perfect weather for his mother's bloody theatrics. Her voice would carry to the far edges of the gathering crowd, and the killing would be easily seen by all, as well. She would have, and had in the past, gone through with the ceremony even if rain poured from the sky. There was meaning in the timing of the offering to the God of Blood. It had all been entirely concocted by his grandfather, of course, but once established, it had become critical to maintain the ritual to keep the masses enthralled. Having been drenched to the skin many times while witnessing the butchery, Balto was grateful for the pleasant night, even if his stomach would be turned before long.

Sitting on one of the carved-rock chairs of prominence, Balto kept his face neutral and his hold on Cariad's hair tight. The boy quivered at his feet. He'd been stoic during supper, nibbling on the bits of food Balto had dropped to him, likely not truly understanding what was to come. Now, though, he knew for a certainty. The sacrificial altar was dark from the dried blood of hundreds of people who'd met their hideous fate there. The rings pounded into the ground around it were obviously used to hold the victim in place. One didn't have to have witnessed a Swarmer ceremony before to picture how it would all play out. The manner in which Balto intended to shield him from the worst of it was nasty, to be sure, but better than the alternative.

The murmurs of the gathering crowd died off the moment when Lilith appeared, dressed in her hooded, red silk robe. Her face was hidden as she walked toward the altar. She was alone, as always, giving an appearance of having communed as the chosen one with their god to infuse his spirit within her. Balto rose with his brother and the other important courtiers who sat to each side. They bowed as one, well-practiced in their designated roles. She waved at them to sit once more before throwing back her hood to reveal her face. His grandfather had always made up his face to look frightening and otherworldly. His mother chose to enhance her already considerable beauty to give herself an ethereal appearance. Men and women alike were enthralled by the vision, and she was free with her body, taking new lovers during the times between the ceremonies. In this extra way, she clasped many of her people closer to her bosom—quite literally. It was those followers who might prove most difficult when the time came to depose her.

From the folds in her robe, Lilith pulled out the ceremonial dagger and held it aloft. The blade flashed in the moonlight. The crowd roared its approval, the sound increasing as the suzerain's personal guards dragged the victim up to the altar. The naked man was upright, stumbling between the men who gripped his arms, yet not struggling. He'd been drugged to make it appear as if the God of Blood already held him in his sway and caused him to go willingly to his death. All the hair on the man had been shaved to purify him for his sacrifice. Nothing marred his skin, having been well-treated, again for the illusion it gave of the ceremony being something more noble than simple bloodlust.

Cariad trembled. "Ambrose." He stared up at Balto with pleading eyes.

Hardening his heart because there was nothing he could do to spare the Moorcondian captain his fate, Balto undid the laces to his trousers, freeing his dick, and pushed Cariad's face at it. The boy resisted, but he was no match for Balto's strength. He focused his gaze on his wife's face to make himself hard enough to push past Cariad's closed lips. Unlike his brother, he had no intention of actually enjoying a blow job while watching the bloody sacrifice. It was merely a way to keep his wife's gaze away from the altar in a manner no one would fault him for.

As Ambrose was bowed over the altar on his back, his hands and feet secured to the metal rings, the crowd quieted again. Lilith raised her knife and began the worn-out speech that never varied, extolling the greatness of the God of Blood and begging him to protect her people and bring them great fortune. As she moved to stand over Ambrose's straining chest, the onlookers began their chant – *blood, blood, blood.* Balto tightened his grip on Cariad's head once more to ensure that he didn't turn around. He didn't push him to take more of his cock, but the boy had other ideas.

Cariad lunged down on it, forcing the head past the tip of his tongue and into his throat. He choked and gagged, his fingers grasping Balto's thighs and digging in. Tears streamed down his face, and still, he didn't stop.

Balto kept his gaze on the altar. He had no choice. It was his duty to watch and relish the moment as his mother plunged the knife into Ambrose's belly, causing the man to scream past the passivity caused by the drugs. His body jerked as Lilith dragged the blade up his chest. Intestines spilled out and blood bubbled up and ran over his sides until Lilith reached down and ripped out the man's still-beating heart. She held it aloft to the increased roar of the crowd, then bit off a chunk and ate it with relish.

This had been one more aspect of his life that had finally set Balto on his course of action. His grandfather had never gone so far. It had all been a theatrical performance to keep him in power. For Lilith, true belief and madness had seeped in. She had helped her aging father to his death with a pillow when the man had fallen ill. No true vessel for the God of Blood would have ever succumbed to a debilitating illness. He had to be gotten rid of, and with her ascent to power, she had embraced the fiction her father had begun and made it a true cause. Only lately had she begun to feast on her victim's hearts. The watching crowd had loved it the first time, and she'd done it ever since. There was no chance this was all for effect. Lilith truly enjoyed the cannibalism. It had to stop.

When Cariad redoubled his efforts, swallowing hard around Balto's shaft, he closed his eyes so that he could picture his wife. He focused his mind on how beautiful the boy was, his soft skin and silky yellow hair. The orgasm ripped through him, closing his hearing to the excitement of those witnessing the butchery of a bound man. For a few glorious seconds, he was lost in the splendor of being pleasured by his wife. But as his climax ebbed, he became aware of Cariad pushing away, sputtering and shaking. Balto let go of the boy's head and watched helplessly as he fell against his legs. He sobbed and shuddered, his chest heaving against the threat of retching. To anyone looking, he was an abused slave, recovering from a hard face-fucking. Balto knew better. His wife cried his eyes out over the horrible death of his former captain and was close to being sick to his stomach.

The ceremony was at an end, though. Lilith smiled at her appeased people. Lifting her hood over her head to obscure her gory face, she glided away on graceful feet. Balto wasted no time in pulling Cariad to a stand and leading him to nearby bushes. The boy dropped to his knees and vomited up Balto's cum and whatever food had been consumed that night. Balto wanted to kneel beside him, holding his hair and rubbing his back. Fury rose in him that he couldn't show his wife that basic amount of tender care. And, of course, Mal couldn't resist coming over and poking at him. Balto clasped his hands behind his back to keep himself from slamming his fist into his brother's smug face.

"An excellent ceremony, wouldn't you say, Balto? The first sacrifice of a Moorcondian—and on such a lovely night. The God of Blood surely favors us."

Malachi didn't share their mother's delusions. Balto knew this, and Mal knew that he knew it. He also understood that Balto couldn't risk denying the belief when so many prying ears were about. So Balto merely nodded with as neutral an expression on his face as he could manage, given how Cariad stayed crouched over, dry-heaving.

Mal looked down at the boy with a sneer. "Still not used to taking your cum? My slut learned to keep it down or get a whipping." So saying, he spun the unfortunate boy around and lifted his shirt to show scars that were barely healed.

There was a purpose to doing so, reminding Balto of their earlier conversation. Balto was sure of it, although other than gaining a valuable slave, he couldn't fathom what his brother's game was. Nevertheless, Balto took the bait. It would please his wife to have the other boy away from Balto's clutches, and at the moment, that was more important than anything.

"I confess my slut's delicacy is tiresome. I will accept your offer of a swap—your bitch for one of the Chainer warriors," he quickly added when Cariad gasped. "I want a horse and basket of salted meat as well. You are getting the better of the bargain, after all."

"Ah." Mal bared his teeth. "Excellent. Which of the slaves do I get in return?"

"Whichever one you want. Tell the slave master I am indifferent to your decision." Even as he said the words, he wondered if that were true. *What is your game, brother dear?*

Mal handed the leash over. "Done. Have a good night, Balto. I imagine you will with two such pretty sluts in your bed…after this one is washed down," he added with a look of disgust at Cariad.

When the man was out of sight, Balto gently tugged his wife to his feet. Cariad stared up at him with red eyes and a runny nose, bits of sick stuck to his lips. Balto used his thumb to wipe them away. "Come. I will take you to someone who will ease your discomfort."

Glancing at the other Moorcondian boy, he added, "Both of yours."

* * * *

Cariad plodded along behind his husband, his stomach still roiling and all his muscles feeling as if he'd run a great distance. He tried to keep the image of a naked Ambrose being led to his hideous death out of his mind, but it kept popping up, no matter what he wanted. At least he hadn't witnessed the man's bloody end, and for that he could thank Balto. He'd known what his husband was up to the moment he'd started feeding him his cock. It had been his own idea to make himself literally sick from the blow job with the hopes that it would blot out what was happening to Ambrose and give him a good reason to cry his heart out and empty his stomach. It wasn't so much a matter of his own pride. Balto had presented him as an image of a thoroughly cowed slave. He was sure any weakness he might show would reflect badly on the man. Of course, that wicked asshole, Malachi, had made an issue out of it anyway. At least it had resulted in Sean being rescued from the evil Swarmer's control.

He reached for Sean's hand and smiled when the boy looked at him. He tried to convey that all would be well with his expression alone. But the poor boy had been brutalized too much. He clutched at Cariad's hand while shooting fearful looks at Balto's back. There were too many people about to say anything, so he had to be content with knowing the boy was safe, even if he couldn't reassure him with words. It wasn't clear where they were going, either. Instead of returning to the castle, Balto was leading them to a small house outside the protective walls of the bailey.

When he reached the door, Balto scratched at it and waited for someone to let him in. Cariad was shocked when it was Tasha who opened the door, Pia squatting on her shoulder. With a smile, she stepped back to let them pass. Cariad walked into a cozy room, simply furnished and with a low fire lit. Once Tasha had shut the door, Balto held his hand out to the monkey. She ignored it in favor of jumping on Cariad's shoulder. It startled him and was also surprisingly soothing to have the creature clamped onto him.

Balto huffed. "Well, I can see I've been displaced by my…slave." He slanted his gaze toward Sean, then gave Cariad a wry grin. "Is your father back yet, Tasha?"

"Yes, I am here." The man came into the room from the back. "You know I race home as quickly as I can after a ceremony." Pele shuddered. "I can't wait for the day when the barbarity ends."

Cariad looked from him, to Balto, to Tasha, to Sean then back to Balto. He let his questions show in his eyes. *Do they know? Can we speak freely in front of Sean?* Out loud, he asked something less provocative. "Pele is Tasha's father, master?"

Balto clapped the man on the shoulder. "He is and, to be frank, he's the only man I can call father, as well."

Pele let out a booming laugh. "By that he means his mother, my mistress, allowed me to show him how to be a man. I'm quite pleased with the way he turned out. Malachi, not so much," he muttered.

Astoundingly, Balto merely grinned instead of dressing the slave down for his impertinence then undid the collars for both Cariad and Sean. The other boy flinched at his approach and rubbed at the red marks where the leather had bitten into his skin. His gaze ricocheted around the room, his fear a palpable thing. Life with Malachi had left him skittish and uncertain of what to do. *No surprise there.*

Fortunately, Balto took charge of the situation. He gestured toward Cariad. "He is in need of a wet cloth and something to settle his stomach."

Pele looked at Tash. "Go fetch what he needs. You know what tea to use."

"Yes, Father." Tasha scurried off, obviously happy to be of service.

Balto turned to Sean. "Take off your tunic." When Sean hastened to obey, he added, "Turn around."

Pele sucked his teeth. "Malachi has a heavy hand."

"He does at that," Balto agreed with a grimace.

"You'll have to tell me later how you wrested the boy away from him. I will fetch my medicinals." The man went in the same direction as his daughter had.

"Sit. Both of you. Not there," Balto added when Cariad started to kneel. "Here." He led him to a worn sofa and lowered him with a touch on his shoulder. Then he carded Cariad's sweaty hair from his face. "You will feel better soon."

His husband went next to Sean, who crouched on the floor. He lifted him to his feet and brought him to a stool by the fire. "Stay here. Pele will be able to reach your back more easily."

Sean sat with his shoulders hunched in and a bewildered expression on his face. Once more, Cariad wanted to reassure the boy that he was as safe as one could be among the Swarm. He held his tongue, though, not sure if the walls had ears. It seemed unlikely. This hut was away from the castle, and its configuration inside so far matched that of the outside. It seemed unlikely that there were any hidden places for spies to lurk. There was, however, the possibility that Sean was here not as a trade but as Malachi's spy. Anyone could be co-opted or brutalized into betraying their own kind.

"Here we are." A cheerful Tasha returned with a mug and a bowl in her hands. A towel was thrown over one arm. She set everything down on the table beside the sofa before handing Cariad the tea. "Drink slowly, now." She soaked the cloth into the water and raised it to wash Cariad's brow.

Balto interjected. "I'll do that."

"As you wish, master." She winked at Cariad, much as her father had done earlier in the day.

Balto washed his face with the kind of care one would hope from a husband. It eased his misery. Even though Cariad had understood everything Balto had done since their arrival was born of necessity, he still had missed their gentle interaction since their marriage. He hoped this horrible matter of seizing control would be over quickly. He wanted this kind man back, not the vicious monster he pretended to be. This was the husband he liked...*even might love*? No, that was fanciful thinking. They were too different, their cultures vastly foreign to each other. An easy blending of their lives was really all that he could hope for. So he sipped his tea and let calmness wash over him with each stroke of the cloth.

Pele returned with a satchel and a wooden box. The latter item he put on another table. He pulled out a pot and began ministering to the wicked-looking lash marks on Sean's back. "Hmm, not as bad as it could be. Mal has been known to beat slaves to death." At Sean's whimper, Pele *tsk*ed. "Sorry. I speak plainly, and if the suzerain weren't so amused by me, my back would be far bloodier than yours."

"I don't understand," Cariad dared to whisper to his husband.

Balto moved closer and wrapped his arm around Cariad's shoulders. He washed his cheeks, chin and neck as he did so. "Pele has been my mother's slave since before I was born. He became my nursemaid. Mal's, too, but he was a horror to the man and broke away from his efforts early on. I didn't. Pele showed me kindness when my grandfather and mother raised us with harshness. He taught me to enjoy reading and instilled in me a sense of honor. His lessons got buried as I grew up, replaced by the training I received to become the Bloodletter. But the kernel of them remained, and it took little for them to push back to the surface and give me strength to do what I must."

"He knows about your plans?"

"Oh yes. He's been instrumental in forming them."

"How does he manage when he belongs to your mother?"

"He's clever, far more than she is. This house is something he convinced her to give him once she permitted him to make a family with another slave…Tasha's mother. She has been dead for a long while, due to illness. And this place has become a safe haven when I need to talk things through with Pele or others. There are no hidden passageways here."

"So you do know about those?"

Balto peered into his eyes. "Yes, because when my grandfather claimed what was little more than a pile of rubble from a long-dead lord, Pele was there to see how he had the masons add in something extra between the walls. People make the mistake of underestimating him. Because he's small of stature, they assume he is small in intellect as well. Nothing could be further from the truth. But their prejudice makes them careless around him.

"He only glimpsed a part of the construction, though. We know some of the entrances but don't know where all of them are or how the passages connect. We have to be very careful, and because we don't know the paths to take, we dare not explore for fear of running into those that use it in furtherance of my mother's rule."

"I've spotted some," Cariad was happy to divulge. "If you take me up to the ramparts and around the outer wall, I can get a better sense of where more are."

Balto smiled and ran his hand down the back of Cariad's head. "My clever boy. You have an interesting and very useful mind."

"That's why I was assigned to the Intrepid." He sipped more of his tea and relaxed into his husband's embrace.

"There you are," Pele announced. "Your back should clear up in a few days' time, my boy. Now, stand and drop your trousers."

When Sean simply remained seated, frozen with inaction, Balto barked out, "Do as he says."

That got the boy moving. He jumped to his feet and let his ragged pants fall to his ankles. Pele parted his ass cheeks and began to apply more of the cream. Wanting to give the kid some privacy, Cariad concentrated on his cup of tea.

"And now that that's done, you'll find sitting a bit easier, I dare say." Putting his pot away in the satchel, Pele eyed Balto. "Stay away from that area until I tell you otherwise."

Balto raised his eyebrows. "Have no fear. I have no interest in availing myself of him in that way."

Cariad shouldn't have been surprised, he supposed. It had been obvious that Balto had secured Sean in order to protect him. Still, his husband's declaration eased some tension Cariad hadn't known he carried. There had been no talk of fidelity. He supposed if he'd stopped to consider it, there was no reason for him to believe that a Swarmer would stay true to his wife. That was especially so given that the idea of marriage itself didn't exist among these people. Balto's next words pleased him even more.

"It would, in fact, be helpful if you kept the boy here at night. I'm sure you can offer him a more comfortable place to sleep than my floor." Balto flicked his gaze to Cariad. "I don't intend to share my bed with anyone but you."

Those words warmed him more than the tea did and settled his nerves, as well. Pele called for Tasha and bade her to take Sean to the sleeping chamber. She had to take the frightened boy by the hand and literally drag him away from his stool and across the room. Before he could think better of it, Cariad jumped up and hurried over to them.

He hugged Sean, holding him tightly when the boy stiffened. "It's all going to be fine, I promise." Then he let go and gave Sean an encouraging smile. Alone with his husband and Pele, he relaxed a bit more. When he went to sit beside Balto again, the slave stopped him.

"Give me the cup and come see what I have. You too, Balto."

Because his husband obeyed the slave's command without question, Cariad did as well. He found himself peering down at the contents of the wooden box Pele had brought in with his medicinals. Phalluses of increasing length and girth, carved out of ivory, lay nestled in a silk lining. Each one had a round base.

Balto barked out a laugh. "Are these what I think they are?"

Pele nodded. "Training plugs. An old man gave them to me when I was younger, mistakenly thinking I was being ravaged by your grandfather. They are meant to stretch one's ass to accommodate a large cock with ease." He flicked his gaze up at Balto. "I assume you are being careful with this boy, unlike the savagery of what your brother had wrought on his former slave."

Balto picked up the smallest one. "Does it really work?"

"I can't speak from personal experience, mind you, but I'm told it does. And it also provides a certain amount of stimulation to the wearer," he added, slanting his gaze toward Cariad. "Use the cream and be careful when inserting it. Keep the box here. Better to not let anyone know you're showing such consideration. You can change the phalluses as quickly as you deem best. Good night, my boy." With that, Pele sauntered off after his daughter and Sean.

Cariad didn't know what to do with himself. He couldn't take his eyes off the ivory penis his husband held aloft. He swallowed hard. "Do you... Will it work?"

Balto smiled. "Let us try to find out."

The man led him over to the back of the sofa and bent him over it. Then he flicked his tunic up to his shoulders and undid his trousers. As with Sean, the clothing fell to his ankles. Cariad didn't move from the position his husband had put him in and felt his own dick rise in anticipation of the fake one being shoved up his ass. *No, carefully placed there*. Balto was considerate, very much so, rubbing the small of his back before parting his cheeks. Something blunt and slippery pressed against his hole, reminding him of Balto's finger prepping him on their wedding night. And as with that time, his husband slid the object in slowly, giving his channel a chance to accommodate the invasion. There was no pain, but Pele had been right—the phallus pressed against his prostate, goosing his arousal.

"Oh," Cariad moaned and tried to hump the sofa.

Balto stopped him with a smack on his ass. "Save that for later, darling boy." He toggled the phallus, making Cariad groan some more, then pulled his trousers and him up. The base of the phallus kept the object from going in any farther and his clothing held it in close to his body.

Balto hugged him from behind. "How does it feel?"

Cariad clenched his hole. "Strange. Like I'm stuffed, except it doesn't hurt."

"Good, because I must get you back to my chambers quickly." He rubbed his groin against Cariad, the hardness of his cock proving that he had been aroused by what he'd done. "Apologies in advance, wife. I won't be gentle."

Chapter Nine

Cariad panted, achingly hard from the hurried journey back to Balto's chambers. With each step, he was reminded that his ass was plugged. It was torture of the sweetest nature. He was glad for it, not only because it pleasured him, but also because it and the ones to follow would hopefully make him able to take his husband's cock all the way. The idea of it thrilled and frightened him in equal measure.

And true to his word, Balto was brusque with him, leading him with that damnable leash, making Cariad quicken his strides to match Balto's longer ones. No one gave them a second look as they raced up the stairs and into Balto's sitting room. A slave knelt by the fire, banking it for the night. She scrambled to her feet and fled when Balto barked at her to get out. Then releasing the collar, he practically dragged Cariad into the bedroom and tossed him onto the down-turned bed.

"Strip!" The man spared him no attention as he tore off his own clothing.

Cariad did the same, not wanting his husband to rip what little he had off his body. His high-handedness was an act for others, he knew, but it was also driven in part by how aroused he was. Balto's cock stood upright, the snake shining with pre-cum in the dim moonlight coming through the window. Cariad's own erection jerked at the sight. Then he was face down on the bed before he knew it, Balto having moved as quick as a real snake would. His husband covered him like a blanket, his hands clasping his shoulders and his head pressed against his. Balto rubbed his hard dick against Cariad's ass, groaning loudly as he did so.

Putting his lips close to Cariad's ear, he whispered, "Scream." He punctuated his command with another bucking of his hips.

Cariad had no trouble obeying. His own orgasm ripped through him, aided by the phallus and Balto's movement causing his own cock to rub against the bedding. He let out the high-pitched yell that he'd held in check all the other times. Here, he needn't be circumspect in his passion. The sounds wrought by pleasure and pain were similar enough that no one listening could know how overwhelmed with happiness he was at that moment. With a roar of his own, his husband followed him over the edge, his cum splashing onto Cariad's back. He reveled in how their skin slid together from the viscous fluid. His only disappointment was that he couldn't take a lazy bath with his husband afterward.

Balto wasn't finished with him, however. He barely slowed in his mimicry of fucking. He thrust against Cariad with an almost frenzy, making them both come again soon. And still the man didn't stop. Long after Cariad passed out from exhaustion, his husband continued to drench him in his cum until at last he was satiated. Cariad was vaguely aware of the man entwining their bodies and covering them with a blanket. They slept as lovers would, and if the suzerain's spies were watching, he didn't care what they thought. And neither, apparently, did Balto. He had to trust that the man knew what he was doing. He really had no other choice.

* * * *

Balto leaned against the outer wall of the ramparts while his wife peered down at the city. They'd made a full circuit of the castle and its walls, inside and out, as casually as he dared. No one could surmise the true purpose of their wanderings, so when others loitered nearby, he played with Cariad as the fuck toy he was supposed to be. A blow job was all they could really do. Even though his wife was stuffed with a phallus two sizes larger than the first one, Balto still dared not fuck him. He wasn't going to do so unless he was sure he wouldn't hurt the boy. With the scrutiny of others bearing witness to it around the castle, he definitely couldn't risk it. In the darkness of his bedchamber, he would be afforded some privacy to take it slowly. Fucking his wife in a corner somewhere was another story. Still, there was a surprising spike to his pleasure playing with his wife in different places. The occasional smirks of passersby didn't put him off, either. He doubted his wife would see it that way, however, so he kept such thoughts to himself.

Cariad pulled his head back. "I've seen enough from this angle." He swayed from foot to foot, a new habit of his.

Does he even know it's to stimulate himself with the phallus? It was hard to gauge, his wife being a reserved person.

The boy gave him a coy look. "Shall I suck your cock to give a reason for us to be taking the air?"

The mere suggestion sent Balto's already aroused dick into a painfully hard state. Saying nothing, he turned to press his back against the wall and widened his stance. Cariad slid to his knees between them with a grace born of practice. He was able to take a lot more of the shaft in his mouth now but had also learned to use his hands to work the rest of it, along with massaging his balls. He gazed down at his wife with half-closed eyes. When the boy peeked up at him, his mouth obscenely wide from Balto's dick, with a coy look shining through, Balto lost it. He could never draw out his pleasure with his wife. He was that provocative.

Cariad dutifully swallowed every drop, another skill quickly learned. Once he returned Balto's cock to its rightful place, he stood with his gaze downcast and his shoulders hunched—the very picture of a beaten-downed slave. His tunic did a poor job of hiding his erection, though. Balto couldn't resist grabbing him close. With one hand he pressed against the phallus, making it wiggle inside Carian's ass. With the other, he clasped the dick through his wife's clothing and jerked. Cariad shuddered and gave a muted cry before collapsing against him.

Balto allowed himself the pleasure of holding him briefly. "Guards are watching," he said as he pushed him away.

Cariad flashed a grin. "Good. Let them see how well you've mastered me...and I you."

"Minx. You like having sex in public, don't you?" The revelation made him want to laugh and hug his wife. He dared not, of course, but there was a funny feeling in his stomach as he looked at Cariad. It wasn't unpleasant, merely...unfamiliar. Dwelling on it disturbed him for some reason, so he moved on to more practical matters. He'd been leaving off the leash as an unnecessary show of control, so he only gestured. "Come. We will go somewhere to refresh ourselves."

Cariad followed him without question, and not all of that was for show. The boy had grown to trust him, he believed. Knowing that puffed up his chest and relieved him of a worry that when it would be most important, his wife might not listen to him. He took him out the back gate of the bailey wall and up a path well-worn by those who knew about it. It took some effort to reach their destination, which alone made it unlikely that unwelcome visitors would intrude. When he reached the hot spring, he parted the foliage obscuring it and ushered his wife through.

Cariad turned in a circle, taking it all in. "This is lovely." He walked over to the pond and squatted to dip his fingers in. "It's warm. Do you bathe here?"

Balto went to join him. "Yes, when the mood strikes. Most of the courtiers and guards are too lazy to bother with the climb. Why would they when there are slaves to heat water and fill a tub for you? Come... Take your clothes off."

He stripped himself and showed his wife where to leave everything, then helped him descend into the pool. They lay with their backs to the rock and here, he was confident of showing affection. He cuddled Cariad in his arms. "Feels good, doesn't it?"

"Yes, and you made me sticky, so a bath is welcome. Although my trousers will need a good washing."

Feeling smug, Balto kissed the top of his head. "Good thing I bought you more to wear."

"Yes. That was kind of you."

The formality of the response irked him for some reason. "It is my duty to provide for you," he said more sharply than he'd intended. "It's in the damn marriage contract, even. You should take it as your due."

Cariad turned to look at him over his shoulder. "I didn't mean to insult you. I…" He cut off his words at the sound of approaching feet and stiffened.

"Don't be alarmed, darling boy. These are my men. This is a secluded place, remember? And there is nowhere for spies to hide."

Amadeus strode up to the spring with the five other members of their inner circle, save Pele, in tow. The men and one woman waved their hands in greeting and were wise enough to give Cariad only a cursory glance. When they were all soaking in the warm water, the meeting began.

"Any sighting of our friends?" Balto asked no one in particular. They were all scouting for him around the island.

It was Amadeus who answered. "None as yet, Balto. Frieda reports there's been no ships on the horizon."

"She is the leader of the fishing guild," he explained to Cariad. There had been precious little time to give him details of the plan. Even Pele's house had become suspect because Sean's loyalties could not be determined with any certainty. His hatred and fear of Malachi was probably real enough. That didn't mean he wasn't being pressured to report what he heard and saw. Malachi might have even promised him freedom in exchange for his help, not that he would ever keep it. "The trawlers are the only boats that go out every day without suspicion. They are looking for Aleki and your ships to arrive at the arranged spot."

"If they ever do," Amadeus said. "They may think it's a trap and have returned to the Chainer ports to outfit their ships with our weaponry instead." There was a general murmur of agreement on that point.

"Aleki would not do that." Cariad spoke with a tone of voice that reminded all of them that he was noble born and a relative of the kai. "He's an honorable man and would not have sent me off to certain death by tricking Balto. I'm sure he's relayed your explosives formula back home to strengthen both fleets, but he will make the rendezvous, as well. The Moorcondian captains will also come, because they too are honorable men." He dropped his chin. "I didn't like Captain Ambrose, but he didn't deserve to die like a slaughtered animal."

While Balto hugged his wife even closer, Amadeus stepped in to smooth things over. "Of course, we meant no disrespect. It's only that we've been at this a long time. We've taken no chances in order to be successful in our venture. We'll only get the one opportunity, and involving outsiders adds an element of uncertainty." He looked at Balto for a confirmation.

"Very true, my friend. We'll give it a few more days, and if needs be, we'll go ahead with our original plan. I had hoped to strengthen our chances with outside help, but we can succeed on our own. Are the marks being readied?"

"Yes, sir."

"What's this?" Cariad tried to twist to look at him face-to-face.

But Balto didn't feel like letting go. The warm water made his wife's skin extra soft. "We have devised a small mark for those who are with us to display on their houses, shops, ships and even clothing. It's simple and shouldn't be noticeable to anyone not looking for it." He sighed. "This is the problem when you are forced to wage war against your own kind. It's impossible to know who is on what side without some indication. And, for security reasons, none of us knows all who've joined, only those we've recruited personally or been recruited by. That way, if anyone falls into the hands of my mother, they can't be forced to reveal the identity of everyone."

"That's wise of you. Show me the mark, please. I need to know, don't you think?"

Balto couldn't argue the logic of it, so he reluctantly let his bride go in order to turn them both to the ledge. He used his finger to draw the circle with the intersecting lines dividing it into quarters.

"What is its meaning?"

"It has none other than Pele created it to mark our allies. That's part of what makes it innocuous."

"You are clever, husband." Cariad erased the image with his own fingers before Balto could.

Enjoying the compliment, yet too proud to take credit, he said, "It was Pele's idea. The man does have a lot of them."

"You'll free him when you succeed, won't you?"

When, not if. The mere fact that his wife said it that way was enough to capture Balto's heart. The thought caused him to jerk.

Cariad placed a palm on his chest. "Are you all right?"

"Yes…fine. Slavery will be abolished once I've prevailed and reestablished order." He cleared his throat and got on with matters. "What has my brother been up to?"

Amadeus shrugged. "Not much, as far as we can tell. He spends a lot of time in his chambers with his new slave. Poor bastard," he added. "The Chainer warrior, not Malachi."

"That goes without saying," Balto said. "Take comfort in the fact that the man volunteered to come. Being fucked by Mal probably wasn't what he envisioned, but when we make our move, he'll be well-positioned to take out my brother. I'm sure he'll enjoy doing so." Balto didn't have to tell any of the men around him that he preferred the Chainer to do it. As much as he hated Mal, he didn't look forward to dispatching the fucker. Blood was blood, and it was already his duty to kill their mother. He wouldn't ask anyone else to do that dirty work.

"Let us relax. There is nothing else for us to do at the moment, and it is a beautiful day for a soak." So saying, he hugged his wife to his chest once more and stared out at the clear, blue ocean. That was where help would come from…or not. He'd gone into this venture believing he only relied on himself and others of the Swarm. If need be, he would make his move with them alone.

* * * *

Cariad and the other Moorcondian boy, Sean, amused themselves by perusing the wares merchants had on display. Balto took his pleasure from watching his wife. Although there was no value in wandering around the city center, it did relieve the boredom of staying in the citadel. He itched to go out to sea, but more than that, he wanted to get on with his rebellion. He would wait one more day, and if Frieda still reported no ships had arrived, he would act. Amadeus and the others were with him on that. Cariad was as well, although more reluctantly. His concern for Balto's safety was something he had no trouble voicing. It was sweet and gave him hope that perhaps his wife cared for him as much as he did Cariad. This feeling was a new one—and odd and uncomfortable—yet he was growing used to it. When the deed was done, he looked forward to spending time exploring it with his wife. If the boy never felt the same way…? Well, life didn't guarantee happiness. He would survive the disappointment and take what he could get from his wife.

The sun was starting to set. "Come," he said reluctantly. "If no trinket catches your fancy, we'll go back to the castle now."

Cariad held up a small cup made of a shiny green stone. A look passed between him and the other boy. "This is Moorcondian." He looked at Balto, his thoughts unreadable, then his eyes widened.

Balto turned to see what had jolted his wife so. His blood froze with the fear of failure that he knew was upon him as Malachi and a half dozen of the castle guards came striding toward them. He turned to Cariad and shoved him away. "Go! Now! And hide."

Cariad hesitated only a moment before grabbing his friend's hand and bolting. The two boys raced away on fast feet, weaving through the crowd. Balto breathed a sigh of relief. Whatever else was to come, his wife had a chance of eluding a similar fate. He knew the town as well as any Swarmer, having studied it from the ramparts. The strange mental gift that allowed the boy to see patterns and recall them perfectly would help him to survive.

"After them." Malachi sent two of the guards in the direction of the boys before stopping in front of Balto. "They won't get far, and if I needed further proof of your treachery born of softness, sending them off gives it to me. You have feelings for the slut." The asshole sneered as he said it, his disgust obvious.

"You will never understand that compassion and kindness makes for a stronger rule than fear and brutality." He didn't bother to struggle as two guards grabbed each of his arms while a third one disarmed him.

"And you apparently are so stupid as to not learn the lessons our grandfather and mother taught us. No matter. Your scheme is thwarted, and you will give me the names of the rest of the traitors. The God of Blood will quench his thirst with them for many nights to come."

"I will tell you *nothing*."

Malachi grinned. "You should have spent more time in the dungeons, brother. If you had, you'd know how futile it is to resist. At least if you cooperate now, you will die on the altar with dignity and for the greater good."

"You don't believe that any more than I do." He was relieved to learn that Malachi only had *his* name. No doubt he suspected Amadeus and the rest of the crew of being in on the plot, but he was being cautious, as well he should. A heavy hand with so many warriors without certain proof might lead to a worse uprising. Taking a good look at the man standing behind

Malachi, he realized how his brother knew of the plan and why he didn't know for sure who else was involved. Only he, Cariad, Aleki and a few of Aleki's advisors knew what had really transpired on board the Chainer ship. To anyone else, it was pure speculation. He sneered at his brother with a toss of his chin. "The Chainer slave is not a whore but a snake in the grass."

His brother smiled. "You don't know this because I would never share my information about the enemy with you when it could benefit me alone. I had made a pact with an emissary of the Chainers. The man was close to their prima kailisa and would have helped us conquer her. Sadly, he was not successful. But at least one of his men survived undetected. I recognized him and knew you'd be foolish enough to part with the mewling slut for him. Such luck, heh? I might actually see the hand of the God of Blood in all of this."

"I've always known you were clever, Mal, and have to give you credit for this turn of events. But I will tell you nothing. And tread carefully, lest you turn loyal people against you."

Malachi flicked his gaze at the men holding Balto. "Take him. You know to where. And won't it be easy to loosen your tongue when I tear your whore apart, bit by bit?"

Balto didn't rise to the bait. He had faith in Cariad and the rest of his men. He only had to hold out and trust them to mount a rescue.

Chapter Ten

Cariad weaved his way through people milling about—down one street, up the next one. He knew what paths to take in order to avoid any dead ends or loops that might lead right back to where Balto had been taken. *Balto.* He couldn't think of his husband, what he might be going through at his brother's evil hands, or risk dropping to the ground and crying. Survival was critical. It was up to him and anyone else in on the plot who hadn't been taken to regroup, find Balto and get him to safety. If Malachi and Lilith ended up dead in the process, so much the better. He found courage in the way the phallus stuffed inside him moved with every step. The sensation reminded him of what was at stake, and it was as if his husband were right there. *Gods, he must not die.* The urgent danger forced him to face something he'd been avoiding—the fact that he was falling in love with his husband. There was no time to dwell on it, though, so he kept going with the single-minded purpose of finding a haven to hide in.

He came to an intersection of two streets populated with various shops and made the split-second decision to turn left. If he went right, they would end up at Pele's house. But that would mean possibly exposing the man and his daughter as traitors. There was no way to know how many of Balto's people had been exposed. Cariad didn't want to endanger anyone. As he ran, he tugged Sean with him. The boy didn't try to ask questions and kept up the pace, having recovered from his injuries, thanks to Pele's ministrations. The guards pursuing them were not as swift. They called out for them to stop occasionally, but it made no difference, of course. Cariad was just glad no one they passed seemed inclined to help their pursuers. At most, they gave the boys curious looks before continuing on with their business.

As they fled past some homes and stores, Cariad tried to see if any of them had the mark. It was hard because, by design, it would be small and not easily noticed. And he didn't have the luxury of slowing down too much. A bakery on their right had its door open. And above it, tucked in a corner was the sign. He nearly whooped with joy. Instead, he abruptly turned into an alley, waited until the customers that had been at the counter left, before racing into the shop. A large woman, wearing an apron covered in flour, eyed them from behind the counter.

"Help," he pleaded in a whisper, then tried to draw the mark in the air for her to see in case she had no idea who he was.

The baker didn't waste any time on questions. Before Cariad knew what was happening, the woman dragged both him and Sean into the back and stuffed them into a pantry. As she closed the door on them, two younger boys and a girl closer to their age peered at them with open mouths. Cariad slid to the floor, taking Sean with him. He tried to be quiet, except his lungs burned from their flight, and he feared they were both breathing so hard and loud that surely anyone out front would hear. No one came. Time ticked by with maddening slowness. Eventually Sean drifted off to sleep, his head resting on Cariad's lap. He dared not sleep, remaining vigilant in case they had to fight and flee again. He had no weapon, of course, and as his eyes had adjusted to the dark, he knew there was nothing but foodstuffs around them. They would be easy to capture. And all the while he sat there, he worried about his husband and what must be happening to him.

Cariad must have succumbed to his own fatigue and drifted off himself, because the next thing he knew, the door swung open again. He startled at the movement, then relaxed a fraction when the girl from the kitchen smiled at him and motioned for him to come out. He shook Sean awake, and they both stumbled past the doorway, blinking against the brightness of the room now lit with a lantern. The girl went to a table set with bread, cheese and what turned out to be a pitcher of water.

"Eat. Then put on these clothes." She picked various items out of a pile. They appeared to be similar to what she and other work-a-day Swarmer girls wore—flowery loose tunics and bits of cloth to wrap around their heads.

Sean spoke through the food he'd already stuffed in his mouth. "You want us to dress like girls?"

"Of course. You can't go out in your own clothing. Your hair alone will give away who you are. No one will pay you any mind if you look like me. With the cover of darkness, hopefully no one will notice the color of your skin. You're too dark for a Swarmer and too light for a Chainer."

Cariad slapped some cheese onto a piece of bread. "She's right." He took a big bite and chewed, even though his stomach was so tied up with worry that he didn't really want to eat. "Everything she says is true, and we can't risk capture after eluding them this far. Where will we go?"

"To Pele's house. My mother is baking extra rolls so that if anyone asks, we can say we're bringing them to the castle. My brothers are already spreading the word to Balthazar's allies."

Cariad swallowed. "You needn't risk your life. I know the way to Pele's house." He tapped the side of his head. "I have the entire citadel mapped out in here."

The girl looked impressed. "That will make you very useful then as the warriors go to rescue our leader. And as for my risk, we are all taking it—and have been for a long time. And without me, if you are stopped, you won't be able to hide your faces. I'll do the talking and you keep your heads down."

Cariad ate more and downed cups of water. Sean did the same. He asked no questions still. Cariad had to be sure about his friend, though. "Are you with us?"

The boy looked startled. With his cheeks full and his eyes wide, he nodded. As Cariad continued to stare at him, he swallowed and asked, "Why wouldn't I be?"

"You spent a lot of time with Malachi."

The boy's pretty face morphed into something ugly. "Yes, I did. And if I have a chance to shove a hot sword up the bastard's ass, I will do it and laugh, as he did every time he made me cry and beg him to stop."

Satisfied that the boy was not working with Balto's brother, he gave him an encouraging smile. When they'd finished eating, the girl stepped out front to give them privacy as they changed. The clothing fit well enough, leading him to believe that the girl had sacrificed her own, given that she was young and small for a Swarmer. They had trouble wrapping the headscarves appropriately and sought her help. Once they were done, they followed her out to the empty front of the store. The baker shoved a basket full of rolls into each of their arms.

"Remember to walk with purpose but no racing to your destination." She went to open the front door and shooed them out. "No dawdling now, girls. Go straight to the castle and don't flirt with the guards. I don't pay you to make moon eyes at boys." Her voice carried out onto the street for anyone nearby to hear. She shut the door behind them.

Cariad and Sean followed the girl. "I don't even know your name," he said softly.

"Alinda," she answered with a toss of her head. "Now quiet. Your accent gives you away."

Because he hadn't considered that and wanted no one's death on his conscience, he stepped back into her wake, keeping his head down. There were many people out and about, although not as many as there had been during the day. It was probably supper time, which made sense, given their pretext of delivering rolls to the castle. No one paid them any mind, and lots of people passing were talking in hushed tones about Balto's arrest. Words like 'dungeon' and 'torture' met his ears, increasing his fear over his husband's fate. He wanted to run to Pele and demand that they move quickly to mount a rescue, but he had to be strong and do what the baker had told him. Any hurrying on his part would call attention to him and the others. That wouldn't do Balto any good.

When Pele's house came into view, he felt a measure of relief. He'd half expected it to be empty or for guards to be surrounding it. None of that was true. Balto had said everyone underestimated the man, conflating size with intelligence. It served them well in this case. The door opened as they approached. Tasha stepped out with Pia on her shoulder and a broom in her hand. As she swept the steps, she smiled at them. "Oh, fresh rolls. Come in, please."

Alinda gestured with her head. "Go make your deliveries to the suzerain's slave, girls. I'll take mine directly to the castle." She sauntered off, although whether she was really heading into that dangerous place, he didn't know.

With a sigh, Tasha literally swept him and Sean into the house and closed the door. "That's a relief. When we got word that Balto had been taken, we feared you two were also lost to us."

Sean smiled at her in an almost flirty way. "We're both fast, and Cariad knew where to go."

Tugging the scarf off his head, Cariad shook his hair down. "I know the streets, that is true. It was lucky I spotted the mark on the bakery, though." As there was no one else with them, he asked the question he feared to. "How many have been taken?"

"Only Balthazar." Tasha got close enough that Pia was able to leap over to Cariad's shoulder. The feel of Balto's pet gave him comfort. When he'd asked why she stayed with Pele and Tasha, his husband had said that his mother and brother hated the monkey, and the feeling was mutual. Pia courted death every time she saw one of them by baring her teeth and screeching. He'd been sorry not to have her at the castle but was glad of it now. She was another piece of Balto to have with him to lend him courage.

"The others will arrive as quickly as they can without causing any notice. My father and Amadeus will lead us now until Balthazar can be saved. There's nothing for us to do except wait."

Cariad was calm by nature and normally good with not having to be active. Then again, he usually occupied himself with drawing. And that thought gave him an idea. "Tasha, do you have a pen and paper I can use?"

"Certainly. What for?"

"I'm going to create a map of the passageways in the castle. It's the only thing I can do right now to help my...Balto." In his head, though, he called the man what he was—*my husband.*

* * * *

Balto grunted as the fist hit his stomach. Really, Mal's men weren't inventive when it came to torture. Did they really think beating the shit out of him would loosen his tongue? He'd taken worse as a boy when he'd fought with his brother. This punishment wasn't going to force him to give up the others. Nothing would, and he wasn't foolish enough to believe that this was all they intended to do to him. Mal's whip dangled at the man's waist, almost alive in its eagerness to tear into his skin. And when that didn't work, there was always the hot poker to sear his skin and implements to pull out his tongue, nails and teeth. Eventually, they would start hacking bits of him off. It didn't matter, so long as they didn't employ their most potent weapon—Cariad. Balto would bite his own tongue off before betraying the people who'd trusted him. And if they'd had that leverage, they'd have used it by now. *Cariad escaped.* Knowing that his wife was safe—for the moment, at least—gave him strength.

He coughed and winced at the pain in his torso and his arms that were pulled wide and high. At least his feet touched the floor. That meant his shoulders hadn't dislocated. Mal had made a mistake there. As soon as he was free again, Balto was sure he could wield a sword, and his first target was standing in front of him, gloating like the idiot he was.

"Had enough yet, Balto?"

"Obviously not, as I've given you no information—nor will I."

Malachi stepped forward to backhand him. "You will or I'll pull out the teeth of that slut of yours. It will make it easier to shove my dick down his throat."

Balto blinked to clear his head. Whatever shortcomings his brother had, he wasn't weak. The hit had scrambled Balto's brains somewhat, but not so much that he didn't know a bluff when he heard one. "If you had him, he'd be here right now. He's too smart for you to catch."

Malachi sneered and took a step closer. "I will have him, in all the ways possible, and you will watch as I do so. Your *affection* for him is as obvious as it is mystifying."

"You will never understand. That's your failing and our mother's. It will be your downfall."

Mal raised his fist again, then lowered it at the sound of someone approaching down the stairs. They both knew who the sharp, mincing steps heralded. Suzerain

Lilith appeared, her ample breasts spilling over her red gown that was open nearly to her navel. She often dressed thusly—as the provocative embodiment of blood. It mesmerized men, and not so long ago, he had been equally enthralled by her raw power and command over others. Now he saw her as the naked evil that she was.

"No progress, I see." Her cool gaze raked over Balto, seeing his sorry state and not being moved by it in the least. He could have been an animal for all that she cared. But then she focused on Malachi. "You disappoint me, son. Then again, Balthazar was always smarter, and it appears, stronger. Now I must add treacherous to those attributes. A pity." Her gaze bore into him. "You will tell us what we want to know, then I will sacrifice you all to the God of Blood. He'll forgive my not using the full moon because of the veritable river of blood I will spill in his name."

Disgust filled him more than fear. "You are barking mad."

Her slap was delivered with an open palm that ended with her claws digging into his skin. "There will be no herbs administered to dull your mind as I plunge my knife into you." She turned with a swish of her skirts and headed back to the stairs. "Get it done, Malachi. I can still make myself another heir if I so choose. Maybe a daughter this time who, unlike her brothers, will not disappoint me."

Mal stood seething until their mother was gone. Releasing the whip from his belt, he cracked it in Balto's direction. "No more kindness for you, brother."

* * * *

Pele's front room was crowded. Cariad sat on the sofa surrounded by people he mostly didn't know. Tasha had taken Sean into the kitchen, neither of them going on the rescue raid in the castle. They hadn't been happy at that news, but Amadeus had taken command and had been resolute in keeping them as safe as possible while the battle to come was waged. Pele was also not there, because his duty was to cater to the suzerain, which meant he couldn't leave her until she allowed it. It was a good thing, however, as they could count on him helping them to get into the passageways. Cariad clutched the rolled-up drawings he'd made of what he knew of the secret hiding places in the caste. There was enough for a few different groups to split up if need be and not have to worry about anyone stumbling around. And Pia remained on his shoulder, a comfort to him. She might also prove useful, hearing or smelling trouble before humans could as they snuck around.

"We need to move now, Amadeus." This from a large woman who smelled faintly of fish. "Balto cannot hold out for long against what those fuckers are doing to him. And I've already sent as many of my trawlers as possible to the inner harbor. Once we give the signal, they will relay it to the foreign ships."

"If they've even bothered to come," a strange man remarked.

Cariad swiveled his head to speak to the room at large. "They will have."

Amadeus cut short any retort. "It is agreed that it's time to act, regardless. Supper will be over, and one can hope the suzerain has dismissed Pele for the night. I know of only one entrance to the passageways, and it's not convenient for stealth. He knows of more hidden-away places."

"I'm sorry I don't know how to get into them," Cariad confessed. "And I can't say that I know where the dungeon is. I only know where it *isn't,* so that we won't waste time going in the wrong direction." He held up his fistful of drawings. "This will help you all do the same if we need to separate."

"Excellent." Amadeus snatched them from him and passed them around. "We stay together for as long as we can, then work in our assigned groups. Anyone other than a slave who confronts you must be killed, unless they show you the sign." When there was a murmur of discontent, he added, "We must harden our hearts at this stage. None of us, not even Balto, knows for sure how many of our people have come to our side. So, we must assume that we are few and that those loyal to the suzerain are many. Once Balto has secured control of the citadel, he can show mercy to everyone else."

"It's war," the fisherwoman said.

There was silence for a while as everyone contemplated what was to come and what they'd be forced to do. Cariad understood how hard this would be for them—to fight against friends and even family. He held no such worries. There was only one person who mattered. *I do love him.* Disaster tended to focus one's mind and allow suppressed feelings to come to the surface. He'd been tamping down his burgeoning love for his husband from the very first night they'd spent together, when the man had caressed his body instead of brutalizing it. Time had confirmed that it wasn't merely gratitude that he felt. He clenched his hole. There had been plenty of opportunity to remove the phallus but he hadn't wanted to. It gave him courage and reminded him of his purpose.

Amadeus nodded toward the men by the door. "Leave. Ones and twos—some out the front, others out the back. Don't be furtive, even pretend you've had a bit to drink, if you want. I saw no one watching the house, but we can't be complacent at this point." He looked at Cariad. "You're with me. Balto will have my balls if I let anything happen to you, but you have to lead us to him."

"I will." He'd almost said, *I'll do my best.* No one needed any caveats in this, however, himself least of all.

He waited as the room slowly cleared out, trying to be patient. When it was his turn, Amadeus grabbed him by the hair the moment they were outside. Pia screeched at the man.

"Forgive me," the man whispered. "Both of you," he added for Pia's benefit, no doubt. "If anyone sees us, I must be able to convincingly say that I have caught you."

Cariad didn't hold back the wince. "I understand so long as you will if I hit you in the balls while I struggle."

Amadeus chuckled lowly. "I can see why Balto likes you so much."

The man's observation shouldn't have warmed his heart. It did, though, as mild as it was, because it confirmed that he didn't merely see Balto's feelings through the lens of his own desire.

Amadeus led them to the back entrance of the castle, keeping to the shadows, yet also keeping up the pretense that Cariad was his prisoner. As soon as they left the house, the monkey jumped off Cariad and scampered beside them. He wondered how much the creature understood about what was happening. *Likely nothing*. How could she? Yet loyalty to her master and those important to him kept her with them. When they approached the gate, the man increased his cruel grip and his stride, acting as if he had every right to be there. Cariad took the sign for what it was and struggled in earnest, dragging his feet and trying to liberate his hair and himself from captivity. But Amadeus abruptly eased his hold as they walked past the two guards there. He nodded to both of them and kept going. Cariad looked for and saw the mark on at least one man's leather vest. Once they were clear, Pia came chattering up to Cariad's feet. He knew what she wanted and bent down to give her access to his shoulder.

They all ended up congregating near the stairs by the kitchen. The tension was palpable among all of them. Everyone was armed except him. That ended when Pele joined them.

The man who Balto thought of as his father gave Cariad a grim, yet determined, look and held out a small knife. "He would not want you defenseless."

With a nod, Cariad took the blade and tucked it into the thin sash that served as his belt. It did afford him a bit more courage, given that he'd been trained in warfare like all boys in Moorcondia had been. He simply hadn't been good at it, but if he were all that stood between Balto and harm, he would put his lessons to their best use.

Pele waved them to follow him. He pulled at a wall sconce and part of the wall slid open. It was an impressive feat of engineering and architecture. Cariad had assumed there were open entrances if one knew where to look, perhaps behind tapestries. The mechanism for this kind of hidden door explained how the existence of the passageways was confined to a few people. It probably meant that there weren't enough spies to listen and watch everyone at once. Balto would certainly have been deserving of observation at least some of the time, however, so he was glad they'd been careful.

Pele gestured for him to bend down once they had all squeezed in and the door shut again. "You lead, and we follow," he whispered. "I can only tell you that the dungeon is somewhere under the main floor. I've never been there. I'm hoping you know the way, given your…gift with mapping."

Cariad answered in the same low voice and gave the man the same information he'd provided the others back at the house. "I don't know where to go. I can only say where the dungeon is *not* as we make our way. Obviously, we go down whenever the opportunity arises."

He decided to hand Pia over to the man, not wanting any distraction and knowing she would be happy with Pele. He gnawed at his lip as he studied the configuration of the passage. It was all so much dark and shadowy stone. Pele lit a small lantern and handed it to him. He raised it high and peered into the distance, seeing almost immediately a fork in the path. Closing his eyes, he called up the map of the castle he had in his head. The charts he made were always for the benefit of others. Everything was fixed in his mind. The images never faded—a gift and a curse, depending on the circumstances. In this case, he was grateful for his ability. Motioning the others forward, he began his journey to finding his husband.

Chapter Eleven

Balto cried out as the lash hit his bare back once again. He'd given up trying to remain silent as the torture continued. It took too much energy, and he imagined his brother liked hearing his screams of pain, thinking he was making progress. Begging would be a nice touch, but he simply couldn't bring himself to do that. His pride could only take so much, after all. It occurred to him, though, that one more bit of humiliation would buy him some time, perhaps enough for his men to rescue him. *Now, there's a thought.* It had been hours since his capture. Surely night had fallen, giving Amadeus and the others the cover of darkness and the quiet that came after supper. With the next strike, he rolled his eyes back and slumped against his chains. He remained still, even as agony shot through his shoulders. And he kept up the pretense through being drenched in cold, salty water. It wasn't easy. Images of Cariad helped him stay strong.

Malachi shouted in frustration, cursing the guards as if they'd been the ones with the heavy hand. "Leave him strung up. I'll be back after I've dined." Heavy, angry footsteps retreated.

There was silence, the guards around him not even talking to themselves. Then a hand cupped one ass cheek. "I wonder what it's like to fuck the son of the suzerain?"

There was chuckling among the others. "It's tempting to find out, although I was hoping Captain Malachi would give us a crack at the Moorcondian whore. I bet this traitor's dick hasn't managed to loosen that tight ass much."

Feigning his unconsciousness was harder to do, listening to this banter. He didn't care what they did to him, but the thought of any of these fuckers getting their filthy hands on his wife and ramming him with their equally filthy cocks… An odd scraping noise caught his attention. He popped open his eyes when he heard the first cry and straightened as he saw his men waging a short battle with the dungeon guards—and winning.

Amadeus' grinning face came into his field of vision. "Sorry we took so long." He looked him over. "You don't look too bad, all things considered."

Balto tried to return the smile, grimacing as everything protested his movements. "Tell that to my back."

Amadeus leaned in. "Tell it to your wife."

As the man stepped away, Cariad popped out of an opening in the stone. The sight of the boy, unharmed, chased away all his fatigue and a good deal of his pain. He barely winced as Amadeus unlocked his shackles and eased him to the ground.

Cariad raced over to him and slid to his knees. "I was afraid we would be too late." Tears swarmed in his beautiful eyes.

Hating to see his wife in distress, Balto tried to raise his arms to take the boy into them. His muscles had other ideas, however, leaving him slumped and breathing hard. "I need a moment to recover, it seems."

"You idiot. You need not put on a brave face for me."

Balto managed to chuckle. "You know nothing about the pride of a warrior. I knew you'd evade them, clever boy. Without you to use as leverage against me, it wasn't so hard to hold out."

"It was possible only because you trusted me enough to tell me of your plans. Is there anything you can do about his pain?"

It was Pele whom the boy asked. The man who had been the making of him walked over with a cup, swirling something into it. And there was Pia. She jumped off Pele to come to Balto. She chittered away as she pawed his leg gently.

Pele held the cup to Balto's lips. "Drink this. It will give you strength and block the pain."

Balto greedily downed the concoction and waited for it to take effect. "What is the status out there?"

"The core of our group waits for us in the passageways to start the uprising on your command. Your boy led us here. We wouldn't have found you otherwise."

Feeling better, Balto managed a wide grin this time. "Of course, he did. I knew he would. It was only a matter of holding out." He staggered to his feet, needing only a little help and forced his body to stand tall. When Amadeus handed him a clean tunic, he insisted on putting it on himself. He shook out his braids, grateful that Mal hadn't thought to cut them off. He wanted to go into battle looking as fierce as possible.

"What now?" Cariad asked.

"We strike first at the head." Balto's stomach clenched from something other than physical pain. As necessary as it was, he hated the idea of killing his mother. He pulled Cariad into a chaste kiss on his head. "I need your amazing mind to lead us to the suzerain's chambers."

Cariad closed his eyes. "The tower on the left if you're facing the front of the castle, yes?"

"Just so."

Taking his hand, Cariad said, "Come on."

Balto followed. "Pia, go to Pele." He figured that was the safest place for her.

He had never been inside the passageways before and couldn't help being impressed. Once he was the suzerain, he would have to decide whether to keep them open or seal up all the entrances. It would be tempting to have a means to spy on those who might plot against him, but he was determined to be the opposite of his family. That meant he had to give up all their wicked methods of governing. These secret parts of the castle would all have to become lost to history.

His wife led them through the maze with impressive surety. They climbed up, circled around some, then up again, until they reached a wall at a small landing at the end of a twisty set of stairs. He didn't need his wife to tell him they had reached their destination. Holding Cariad and himself to one side, he gestured to Pele to find the release that would let them out. The man ran his fingers around the edge of the stone and pushed. Balto tucked the information away in case he needed to get in and out on his own. A part of the wall popped open with barely a whisper of sound.

His stomach clenched once more as he girded himself for what he had to do. Pele's concoction gave him strength, and his goal of freeing the Swarm from his mother's evil grip allowed him to harden his heart. Gesturing to the others to remain, he stepped out of hiding, his sword at the ready. It had belonged to one of his torturers. Now it would be used for the greater good.

Balto found himself in the far corner of his mother's bedchamber. It was meant to be a means of escape, no doubt. She wasn't in bed, but he could hear her speaking to someone from somewhere beyond the archway on the other side. He walked silently as his grandfather had taught him to, surely never expecting the skill to be used against his own daughter. Keeping to the wall, he peeked around the corner. His mother knelt before a small altar, a disemboweled animal of some sort lying open and dripping blood. She chanted to the God of Blood, then held an organ to her mouth.

Disgusted and reminded that she was too far gone to reason with, he stepped out into the open. "That is the last sacrifice you will ever make, madam."

Lilith whirled around, jumping to her feet as she did so. Gore coated her lips, and when she smiled, bits of flesh were stuck between her teeth. She laughed maniacally. "Father was right. The God of Blood blessed you with intelligence and courage. How unfortunate that you turned it against the One who provides for us all." She took a step toward him and pulled a knife from the folds of her gown. "Your blood will run here and now in a special glory to His greatness."

Balto raised his sword. The woman was too blinded by her hubris to understand that with his longer arm and blade, he would skewer her before she could plunge her knife in. And if she threw it...? Well, he was quick, despite the torture. He would be victorious, he had no doubt. All he needed to do was take the next step. Something made him hesitate. This was hard, far harder than he could have imagined. And he wasn't the Bloodletter anymore. A lot of his transformation could be credited to his wife. The compassionate boy had worn away what viciousness had remained inside him.

There was a quick movement past him—Pele…and Pia. The man had always been fast on his feet, regardless of the length of his legs, and the monkey ran on all fours after him. He raced to Lilith and dropped to his knees in front of her. "Your worship. Please forgive me. My loyalties were tested, and I failed you." He held up his knife. "I give myself freely in service to the God of Blood."

Lilith stared down at him, her knife poised, distracted by the drama unfolding. "Do it!"

"No!" Balto couldn't bear the sight and moved forward, knowing that it was already too late to stop it.

At that moment, Pia made herself known to his mother. With a screech, the monkey launched herself using Pele's back and grabbed Lilith by her face. The woman shrieked and batted the animal away. Pele took advantage of the distraction and struck without hesitation, his knife being buried to the hilt, not in his own heart but in Lilith's stomach. As the woman stumbled back, he followed her, dragging the knife up her torso. When she landed on her back, he straddled her and continued until the knife hit her heart. "Take comfort in going to the god you love so much that you would have destroyed your people to appease him."

"Pele." Balto lowered his sword and grabbed the man, pulling him back from the body. He held him tight as he'd done as a boy and upset about his life, comforting Pele now instead of the other way around. "Let's leave." He was prepared to drag the man, if necessary.

Pele surprised him by pulling away, scooping up Pia and walking purposefully toward the secret door. "I was always going to find a way to be the one, you know. No man should have to kill his own mother, even if she had killed her own father."

Balto caught up and gripped the man's shoulder. "There are no words to express how much I owe you…*father*." He'd finally found the courage to say the word he'd thought so many times before.

"A son never has to thank his father for protecting him."

Blinking back tears he couldn't afford to shed, he followed Pele into the passageway and gathered Cariad tightly into his arms. He needed the warmth and softness the boy represented. "You must go with Pele, darling boy, back to his house. It's the safest place to be while we do as we must."

Cariad stiffened. "I'm not leaving you."

"We can find our way without you now. You're not the only one with a good memory."

Cariad tried to push away. "Oh, you stupid man! Do you not understand that I must stick by your side because I love you. These last few hours, not knowing whether you lived or died, were torturous for me. I need to stay with you. *Please*." He held on tight now.

Ridiculously pleased to hear those words, Balto was at a loss for his own, especially given the audience they had. Instead, he pressed their bodies together and cupped the boy's ass. Another surprise made him smile. "You're still plugged," he whispered in his wife's ear.

"Of course I am. It's like a piece of you has been with me all along. Please don't send me away."

"Very well." Balto let go, reluctantly. "Stay behind me, take no foolish chances and if I tell you to run, you run. Understood?"

"Yes, master." Cariad's dimples showed in the dim light.

Balto's cock stirred, despite the day he'd had. Ignoring it, he rounded on Pele. "That goes for you, too."

Pele nodded. "I'm here to obey you, suzerain."

Strange as it was to be called that, Balto could feel the rightness of it. "Let's go. Malachi is next."

* * * *

Cariad's lungs burned as he ran full tilt to keep up with his husband and the others. Now that the fight had left the castle to be continued throughout the citadel, they had to cover a lot of ground quickly to remain in control. The sun had long since risen, and Malachi still had not been found. His chambers had been empty, so Balto had decided to clear the large structure of as many of his brother's loyal men as they could. It was slow going, the passageway allowing them to strike without warning before retreating into the mostly secret rabbit warren. A few soldiers surprised them by knowing how to penetrate the area. Pia had alerted them to their presence each time. It was tight quarters, but Balto's men quickly dispatched them. And although not even Balto knew how many had been converted to their cause, it turned out that a lot had. There were more allies than not, when all was said and done. Those courtiers who were out for themselves and therefore agnostic when it came to their leader, understood easily that loyalty to Balto meant survival.

In the city, most people hid behind closed doors. The fisherwoman had left the castle early on in the fight to send off the first signal to the ships that the fight had begun. Even within the thick walls of the palace, Cariad heard the sound of a massive firework going off. Other fishing ships raced to relay the message farther out with their own fireworks. It was a system not unlike lighting fires along a route to send a simple warning. Moorcondia had used if for years on land. He hoped Aleki and the others were in place to see it and help. He had no doubt they would come. The question was whether the wind had favored a quick journey. There was no way to know, but now that they entered the dock area, he could tell it was blowing strongly this day.

Balto stopped abruptly and gestured toward the harbor. "As we thought, Malachi hopes to make his escape out to sea. Coward." He spat on the ground.

It didn't surprise Cariad that Balto's brother had turned tail. It had always been about power for that man, not belief. Balto himself had told him as much. Self-preservation was key for someone like that. Left alone, he might never come back, turning pirate instead. Balto couldn't take that risk, however. There was no surprise that he turned to head to his own ship.

His loyal sailors were already there. "Get under sail as quickly as possible!" Turning to Cariad, Balto grabbed him by the shoulders. "I assume there is no point in my saying you must stay here."

"None whatsoever." Cariad kept his gaze steady so that his husband could see his resolve. He gestured toward Pia. The small creature had kept up with them the whole way and now squatted by his feet. He didn't want to leave her behind. "She's coming, too."

The man gave in quickly. "I suppose you both might be safer with me, and if the God of Blood really did exist, he'd know I'm always better with you at my side."

Cariad couldn't help staring at him, his mouth wide and stunned into silence. It wasn't exactly a declaration of love, but he'd take it. His heart pounded with something other than fear and breathlessness as he waited for Balto to give orders to the others.

"Amadeus, I need you onboard." He dropped to one knee. "Pele, please stay here, get the castle in order as best you can. If I…if I don't prevail with Malachi, you will be the new suzerain. You are respected," he added when Pele shook his head. "People admire you, whether you know that or not. I would trust no one else to carry on my hoped-for legacy."

Pele reached out to hug Balto. "I shall not let you down. And you will return victorious. Remember, Malachi's greatest weakness is his pride. He will want to fight you instead of staying on course to get free."

"I know." With that, Balto stood, grabbed Cariad's hand and hurried up the gangplank.

* * * *

Mal had always picked his sailors based on who kissed his ass the most. Balto had looked for skill. Catching up to him was easy. They'd barely passed into open waters before they were close enough for him to make his point.

"Amadeus, one shot over the bow, if you please."

He held onto Cariad, who stuck to his side as he'd commanded, as the cannon boomed. The ball flew across the water and Mal's ship to splash on the other side. Mal proved smarter than he expected, at least for the moment, and kept to its course.

Amadeus handed him a spyglass. "Their sails aren't trim enough for maximum speed. Shall we fire another shot?"

"Keep on their tail. The farther out we go, the less chance he'll want to return to the citadel." He didn't add *if we fail*. In his heart, he knew they would succeed, but being cautious was always smart and had done him the favor of heading in the direction where the foreign ships should be—if they'd come. He glanced down at his wife. They wouldn't abandon Cariad. Of that he was certain.

As they closed in on their quarry, Malachi's ship tacked suddenly, presenting its side. "Incoming!" He shouted the obvious warning before shielding his wife. Mal wouldn't fire a warning shot.

The first ball missed them. The second did not, shredding one of the sails. But his sailors didn't need to be told what to do. They brought the ship around and returned a volley that hit their target in multiple places. Then the fighting began in earnest. Around and around they went, tacking away, shooting iron balls with each turn. He'd played this game many times with his brother, although always in tandem to destroy the ships of others. He judged that he had the upper hand—only just. Skill was critical. So was luck occasionally—and that could favor either of them.

Cariad dug his fingers into his arm. "Look!"

Balto followed his wife's pointing and just beyond the horizon, another ship approached. Then another. And another. "Our signals reached the kai."

"Don't be so surprised. It was your brilliant plan and it worked. All of it did."

"Ease off, Amadeus, and hoist the white flag. We wouldn't want our allies to mistake us for enemies."

"What if Malachi also raises one?"

"He won't. Pele was right. The asshole has too much pride to possess a white flag, let alone use one."

As he stood with his legs braced and his wife against his side, Balto watched his brother's demise unfold. The Chainers and Moorcondians had cleverly rigged contraptions to their decks. They spewed iron balls clumsily at Malachi's ship. They weren't as effective as the broadside cannons, but with three ships keeping up a steady barrage, they managed to decimate the sails and put holes on the deck and through the stern. The ship was already listing when the fighting stopped.

It was not that Malachi gave up. It was more that Aleki and the others were too decent to slaughter those still alive. Balto was tempted to sail closer again, yet knew his brother could be using a ploy to get him to do just that. Losing would be more palatable to the man if he took Balto with him. Nothing happened for a long while, except occasional screams coming from dying sailors who deserved some pity, even though they'd thrown their lot in with a bastard like Malachi. Then someone climbed the railing, holding onto a broken mast.

A ball formed in his stomach. "Amadeus, my spyglass." He hesitated to look through it once it was in his hand. There was no doubt as to who stood over the water. As he focused the lens on his brother, the asshole smirked. *He must know I'm watching.* Opening his arms wide, Malachi plunged into the ocean. His head bobbed up a time or two before sinking into the depths for good.

Cariad hugged his waist. "Oh, Balto, I'm sorry."

Biting back at the pain screaming ever loudly from every place that had been beaten and whipped, he gathered his wife close. "No need to feel badly for me, darling boy. I am the luckiest of men, for I am free of my mother and brother without having to do the bloody deeds myself." He couldn't bite back a groan. "And now I must sit, because Pele's magic potion has worn off."

His ass hit the deck with a jarring thud, causing his vision to wink out for a moment. But Cariad was there, peering at him with concerned eyes and caressing his face. "Stay with me, my love. We'll patch you up and put you to bed. You need the rest. Let others do the work now."

Balto was not so weak that he couldn't cup his wife's chin with one hand, ignoring the ache in his shoulder as he did so. This was too important. No doubt he'd survive, but just in case, he had to let his wife know. "I'm lucky not only because my evil family is gone, but also because I have a new one— a good one. *You,*" he clarified when Cariad blinked in confusion. "I love you, too. Who would have thought that a map-making doxy would pull out of me feelings I didn't know I was capable of having. I will be a good husband to you, Cariad, as well as a fair ruler. Now kiss me quickly before I pass out."

As his wife's soft lips brushed his own, he fell forward, knowing that he would be caught.

Epilogue

Cariad lay naked on his stomach as Balto teased the phallus out of him. "I'm glad you chose to keep these chambers. I don't think I could ever get comfortable in your mother's." He shivered at the thought. "It's worse than the dungeon." Balto fucked him slowly with the phallus, humming in appreciation as he no doubt stared at Cariad's hole. "Are you listening to me, husband, or has all the blood gone to your dick?"

Balto shoved it in hard enough to make Cariad squeak. But his dick loved it, nearly releasing his cum. Then the man pulled it out just as fast, leaving Cariad feeling empty. His hole spasmed with desperate need to be filled again.

Balto flipped him over. "Pele has emptied it of all remnants of her. It's his to do with as he likes, although I doubt he will live there, either. I may seal it up, along with the passageways." He spread Cariad's legs with his knee, pushing them up to expose his ass. "Are you sure about this?"

Cariad let his passion show through. There were no more barriers between them emotionally, and he wanted none physically, as well. "I want this. I'm ready for it. Fuck me with your real dick, Balto."

"It's been a different kind of torture, not being able to play with you while I recuperated. This will mark the beginning of our future together more than anything else." He grabbed the pot of cream and slathered it over his cock.

Cariad worried somewhat that his husband was pushing himself too soon after his ordeal. But he'd been out of his bed the very next day after their successful coup. No one could stop him from seeing to every detail of the new order in the citadel himself. Cariad had followed him like a chick, but so had Pele, the man clucking at Balto like a mother hen. And blessedly, the man had wonderful medicinals that healed the many injuries and kept Balto's energy up.

That was done now, though. Clasping his knees, he pulled them up as close to his face as he could manage. He wanted to show his husband how much he trusted him and to feel every inch of that cock as it slid into him.

Balto smiled as he positioned the head of his dick at the puckered entrance. "I won't last long…this time." As he'd done before, Balto clasped Cariad's dick and jerked him while he fed his cock into Cariad's ass. It was tight, the phallus training notwithstanding, the girth of the man having no equal. Cariad relaxed and pushed out, a suggestion of Pele's. It worked, helping the cock to enter more easily, and the moment it brushed against his prostate, he came with a rush and a scream. It was the best orgasm he'd ever had, and it chased away what little pain there was.

Balto kept going, slowly yet with no hesitation. When Cariad could open his eyes again, his husband was flush up against him. His ass was stuffed to the point of bursting, but nothing had ever felt so wonderful. This was where he'd been headed for a long while. He simply hadn't known it. "I belong to you."

Balto began thrusting, shallow at first, then with longer, faster thrusts. He jerked Cariad to completion again and came with him, that great cock swelling and coating his insides with warmth. Balto bent over and kissed him while they remained joined. "And I am yours, my darling boy. My love."

* * * *

Later he lay in his husband's arms, too spent to move. His mind had come back to life, though, and he couldn't help thinking about the future. "I can't wait until Aleki returns to finalize the treaty. He's promised to bring Carwyn, and now that we're both married men, we'll have more to talk about."

"Hmm. I'm happy to meet your brother, of course, but do you intend to speak about our bed sport?"

"I certainly do! I bet your dick is bigger than Aleki's. Don't you want me bragging about your prowess?"

"It seems…undignified. I'm a head of state now. A certain amount of decorum should be maintained." His tone was serious, but he couldn't keep from chuckling. "Well, maybe you can gossip a little about me." He hugged him closer. "I'm glad you enjoyed me."

"It was amazing, and although I was determined to take all of you at some point, I must thank Pele for his excellent advice. And I'm glad that Sean has elected to stay. I think he and Tasha make a lovely couple. Do you think Pele is pleased with the possible union?"

"I'm sure he is. The boy held up when it mattered the most."

They lay quietly some more, then Balto rolled them over to face each other. "I will do what needs to be done to settle the Swarm and make it into a peaceful and prosperous race for however long it takes. I'm not certain, however, that I will make a good leader in the long run."

Cariad nearly scoffed at the idea, then gave it some thought. "I can see how you might be right about that. You are happiest at sea, aren't you?"

"Yes. You know me so well."

"Who would replace you? Oh, Pele." The answer was obvious. "Will they accept him, do you think? He's been a slave, and your people seem to value size."

"Both are true. I've made him my chief advisor. Everyone will get used to seeing him in a position of power. It will take time, naturally, but I would like to journey to uncharted waters. Pele, himself, comes from a land near here that I have never visited. It's where the spices we use so liberally come from."

"Oh, that scent is one of the first things I noticed about you—that and your hugeness."

"As long as both please you." He hesitated. "Will you come with me?"

Cariad poked him in the stomach. "And where else would I be but by your side?"

"I've already taken you far from your home and family."

"Have we not just established that we are each other's family now? I would like to go back to Moorcondia, of course, for a visit. Perhaps that is where we venture first? Then the world will be ours to go where we like, and maybe we see what no one has before. We'll take Pia with us, won't we?"

Balto's face broke into a wide smile. "We will, yes. She's family, too. If I needed a reason to love you more, this will do nicely. Together we can do anything… *wife.*"

"*Husband.* Now, fuck me again…if you can."

Ever the warrior, Balto rose to the challenge.

Want to see more from this author? Here's a taster for you to enjoy!

Treaty Brides: The Brigand's Bride

Samantha Cayto

Excerpt

Evander had to choke back a whoop of excitement as he spied the carriage rumbling down the road. He and his men hadn't had such fruitful pickings in a long while, and though summer it may be, fall and winter would come soon enough. This ambush might yield considerable provisions for those in need to get through the hard seasons ahead. He swung down the thick branches of his favorite perch and landed with a thud on the forest floor. Every bone in his body protested. *I'm getting too old for this.* It was no more than a passing thought. He couldn't stop, because the misery of those unable to protect themselves hadn't—and likely never would.

Nemo, his second in command, appeared out of thin air. They had a way of blending in with their surroundings. Despite their years together, Evander could still be startled by them…and that was good thing. If one wanted to lead a band of brigands, it helped to have someone for whom stealth was second nature. Nemo's short and thin stature was an asset, as well. It made it easier for them to hide behind trees and rocks, unlike Evander's tall, broad frame. Even a mountain would have trouble providing him cover. It hardly mattered. Here was where people in need depended on him, so this was where he'd stay. *And probably die.* But he never dwelled on such matters. His life meant nothing compared to the hundreds of others he served.

Nemo stood with their legs braced and arms crossed. "Someone is looking pleased with himself."

"Ha!" Evander clapped them on the shoulder. "Some rich person rides this way and without any outriders. I saw only one coachman and a footman on top."

"Soldiers could be hiding inside, ready to spring a counter ambush when we stop them." That was one of the better things about Nemo. They always assumed the worst.

"Unlikely, as the coach is too small. The most it could carry is four people. Hardly a challenge for us."

"I'll line up extra men, just in case."

"Fair enough."

As soon as Nemo disappeared back into the woods, Evander climbed the tree again to keep track of the coach's approach. Whoever was inside, and whatever the reason for them to travel this stretch of road that had gained a reputation of populating highwaymen, their pace indicated they were in no hurry. That was all to the good. It would allow Nemo to get everyone into position with time to spare. He was confident he'd arrive as usual to do the greeting, even if he stayed a bit longer to watch the carriage's progress. There was something about it… "Well, fuck me."

This was a chance he'd been hoping for since the last harsh winter. Simple robbery was no longer lucrative enough to satisfy the needs of those he helped. The dire situation required a bolder move, one that would produce far more coin in one fell swoop. It would be a tremendous escalation of their work, but one he wasn't completely comfortable with—nor had most of those who followed him been when he'd first broached the topic. Thieves, robbers, runaways and conmen they may be, but none of them had experience in what he now planned. The memory of all those starving faces from around the surrounding villages and farms helped him to harden his heart, however.

He scrambled down the tree and raced to the spot where they would employ their ambush as shadowy figures—members of his band and loyal to him, one and all—arrived to take their positions. This time, he was going to ask much of them, and he wanted to have time to set them on the right path. It was going to be difficult, he knew. Nemo and the others turned to look at him with surprise as he raced to join them. It wasn't in his nature to be rushed, but this situation wasn't normal. And he wanted to deliver the news as good fortune.

"The carriage belongs to the baron." He stood grinning with encouragement while his men absorbed the information and understood its importance.

Maurice was the first to get it. That was no surprise, given the man was high-born, even if it was on the wrong side of the blanket. He had a sharp mind that was as good at tactics as Nemo was with logistics. "Our first chance for abduction has arrived, then. I wonder who's inside." The man had a face not unlike a hedge fence, but when he smiled, his blue eyes crinkled in an appealing way.

Evander shrugged. "Who, indeed? Someone worthy of a carriage instead of a wagon or a saddle-sore ride through the woods."

The information finally clicked for Nemo. "It could be no one of great importance. Maybe the tax-collector has broken his leg and needs a carriage to get around for his dirty work. For his own purposes, the baron would certainly want his man to do his duty quickly."

"Possibly," Evander allowed. He didn't think so, however. That particular man was smart enough to know this road was a danger to him. They'd robbed him often in the early years. There were others that, while inconvenient, provided a safer route, and the tax collector had taken to using those. "We can only know by doing what we do best, and once we do, I'll make a decision of how to proceed."

"You mean to take the occupant hostage and ransom them." This from Brother Manfred. The man was dressed for battle as usual, with his short sword tucked into his belt looped around his robe that served as a tunic. But his role was only ever to soothe frayed nerves as their victims were liberated of their wealth. His kindly face, lined with age and accented with a meticulous goatee, helped travelers believe it when they were told they wouldn't be harmed. His obvious tie to the nearby monastery helped, as well, although if they only knew what went on in that dark place, they wouldn't feel so calm around him. Fortunately for all of them, Manfred had fled the naked cruelty and avarice of the monastery. He was the most decent man Evander had ever known and the keeper of his band's collective conscience. That was the problem now, regrettably.

"I do," Evander confirmed. "The person in that carriage may be our first and only chance at extorting a sufficiently large amount of money to see our people through the coming winter. It's a happy circumstance if it comes from the baron, himself, and not one of the fawning nobles he rules over."

Manfred shook his head. "I've been against this scheme since you first contemplated it, as you know. Robbery is one thing, but kidnapping crosses the line. How do we look ourselves in our own reflections, never mind explaining it to those whom we help?"

Nemo spoke up. "When it means their children are not starving, they won't care. It's not like we're going to kill anyone."

Manfred frowned. "What if the occupant is a woman? How will she fare, living rough in the forest with us for the many days it will take for a ransom to arrive?"

Evander tried not to sigh. They had had this discussion, or variations of it, before. Every issue Manfred raised was a valid one. They simply paled in comparison to the suffering of so many others. "Mabel and Cath manage, as well as the rest of us." He gestured toward the women, who stood ready with their bows. "And Susannah will know how to make a female guest comfortable." The keeper of their camp was a strong woman for all her tender years and soft demeanor.

"You'll get no argument from me about the strength and skill of our female comrades, Evan. They are not, however, noblewomen, as any woman in that carriage is likely to be. She will be used to finery and pampering and not, frankly…shitting in the woods."

"She'll get used to it," Mabel interjected. "It's not that hard—not as much as being beaten and raped." Like many of his 'men', Mabel had fled from an untenable life, where living rough in the forest and robbing passersby was a glorious life in comparison.

Putting his hands on his hips, Manfred shot her a sympathetic look. "I should hope we can do far better than that in our treatment of others." He turned his attention back to Evander. "I have a bad feeling about this."

Evander put a hand on the man's shoulder. "I understand your concern, and I can't say I am entirely happy about the idea myself. I don't want any of you to do that which your conscience cannot abide. Let us make a compromise and agree that if the occupant of the carriage is a woman, we take her money and nothing else. If it's a man"—he closed his eyes a moment—"we have to do more to help our people."

Maurice clapped his hands and rubbed them together. "A fine plan, Evan." He glanced around at the others. "Well, what are you waiting for? Get into position, everyone." There was only a moment's hesitation before the rest did as Maurice said.

Evander squeezed Manfred's shoulder. "Are we good, Brother?"

The man nodded once. "Aye, I suppose so, but I still think this is a mistake. Bringing a stranger to our camp will be dangerous, and he'll require constant guarding."

"Agreed." Evander let go. "And as this is my idea and my responsibility, I will look after our guest in all ways. If it fails, it will be my fault and no one else's."

"I can only pray to the gods that we will succeed."

Relieved that there was no more disagreement on the matter, Evander said, "I thought you no longer believed in the gods." *And who would, after what you witnessed in the monastery?*

"I don't, but it doesn't hurt to ask for help, just in case."

With a laugh, Evander headed to his usual place in an ambush, pushing away the doubt he felt in his heart.

* * * *

Rory stared out at the endless monotony of the forest. He'd never been so far from home, yet he found nothing exciting about his trip. It was boring and uncomfortable. His father had only spared the oldest carriage he had, with weak springs and lumpy seats. And what he expected to find at the end of the journey didn't give him any hope of something better. He expected University City to be more frightening than anything else. Still, tedium was the immediate problem. "Will we never get there?" He didn't bother to hide his peevishness. He was still within his father's reach, and everyone expected such an attitude of him, anyway.

His valet, Maxwell, gave him the sort of stern look that he employed with impunity. "We've been gone less than two days, sir. It takes at least five to get to our destination."

Rory rolled his eyes. The old man was tiresomely right—always—and never shied away from delivering hard truths. There was some comfort in the routine, and it would be much harder to make the journey without him—not that Rory would ever admit such a thing. As far as he was concerned, Maxwell was just as guilty about the misery that his life had become as his parents were. It might not be fair to blame a servant, but the man was the safest place to concentrate his anger. "You might have devised a way to amuse me while we plod along."

"Would you like me to sing some bawdy tavern songs? I know quite a few." The old man's face remained as placid as ever.

Rory dismissed his ridiculous question with the scoff it deserved and went back to staring out of the window. This forest sitting on the outskirts of his father's holding was vast, dark and foreboding. No human with an ounce of sanity would make their home there, given that it was populated with all manner of large and dangerous creatures—or so he'd heard. Still, it held a certain fascination. A person could leave the known world behind and lose themselves within its thickness. *What would happen if I jumped out of the carriage right now and ran into those woods?* Would his father's men even bother to stop and chase after him? *Probably not. Good riddance to him,* that's what they would think. Well, perhaps Maxwell might do so, out of loyalty to Rory's dead mother, if nothing else.

Shaking his head, Rory dismissed the impulse. It never helped to imagine a life other than the one he was leading. "Do you think there are monsters living in the forest?" It was a silly question, but he was bored.

Maxwell drew in a breath, a clear sign that his patience was being tested. "There are no monsters, sir."

Rory was considering a retort about how that was wrong, as he'd lived with a few his entire life, when the carriage lurched to a halt. Shouts penetrated the glass window of the door. He grabbed onto the edge of his seat. "What's that? What's happening?"

Grim-faced, Maxwell peered outside. "Brigands, sir."

"We're being robbed." It wasn't a question, but others bounced around his mind, mostly concerning whether this outcome had been the plan all along when he'd been sent on the journey.

The door opened abruptly, revealing a sharp arrow notched and pointing generally in his direction. "Everybody out, if you please." The voice issuing the order was surprisingly cultured, not the rough speech of a workman. A large hand with long fingers that didn't belong to the archer beckoned them. "Now, if you please. Otherwise, I'll have to come in and drag you out." The tone of the man implied that he would find such a move bothersome.

Before Rory could make himself move, Maxwell leaned forward and climbed out of the carriage. "If it's money you're after—and I can only assume it is—I have access to it." The man uttered a muffled grunt of outrage and disappeared from Rory's line of sight.

That hand reappeared and beckoned again. "Your servant is not enough. Come now. My patience is wearing thin."

Rory had long ago mastered the art of hiding his fears and using contempt to deal with bullies. He forced himself to step out of the carriage with his head held high. His fast-beating heart made it hard to maintain his expression of distain, but he could do it. A façade of indifference was his only defense. His well-honed control stuttered to a halt when he saw his attacker for the first time. A man much older than he, yet still significantly younger than Maxwell, stood with his hand on the hilt of a sheathed knife. Tall and broad, the brigand was an impressive man, even though he wore a tunic and trousers that had seen better days. Dark brown hair hung in shaggy layers nearly down to his shoulders. His unkempt look showed no signs of having lived a life of luxury. Although his clean-shaven face didn't have the florid and soft look of Rory's father, his weathered skin was nevertheless smooth-looking, and his brown eyes were clear. When he smiled at Rory, he showed straight, white teeth. This was no ordinary highwayman.

"Thank you for joining us, my lord. It's such a lovely day, much better to talk outside than in that stuffy carriage."

"I'm not a lord." Rory bit out the truth from habit. Folding his arms, he tried to give the man a look of distain. It was hard to do so. There was something compelling about the brigand that disturbed and cowed him. Rory didn't want to stare into his eyes.

"I beg your pardon." The man gave him a baiting smile, then tapped the outside of the door. "This is the baron's crest, is it not?" When Rory said nothing, he continued with a narrow-eyed gaze. "The baron has three sons, I believe."

Rory tugged at his frizzy braid, not sure how to respond. But anyone who had ever seen the baron knew that Rory's curly, red hair was not usual. His pale skin, dotted as it was with freckles along the bridge of his nose, made him an outlier among his family, as well. "Do I look like a son of the baron?"

"Yes, actually." The brigand startled him by flicking a finger at Rory's sleeve. "Such fine dress speaks of nobility." He used that same finger to catch Rory's necklace and give it a gentle tug. "And this jewelry is worth a pretty price."

Rory wrenched away. "Don't touch that!" His abrupt movement would have sent him tumbling to his ass on the carriage step if the brigand hadn't caught him by the elbow. Rory pulled free. "And don't touch me!"

"My apologies, sir. I didn't mean to alarm you. We don't steal that which has obvious sentimental value. We seek money, first and foremost."

Rory clasped his palm against the necklace. *How does he know what it means to me?* "My valet has already told you he keeps the coin. It's in the strongbox up with the coachman. Take what you want, and let us go on our way."

"Why, thank you very much, kind sir." The man's tone mocked, but his eyes twinkled as if Rory were in on the joke and not the butt of it. "We've already liberated that. There is something else, however, that will fill our coffers even more."

"Wh-What are you talking about?" He didn't like the look in the man's eye.

"You."

"Me?" Rory's voice squeaked, which was embarrassing but he was too shocked to care. "You can't be serious."

"Oh, but I am. You are the baron's son, of that I'm sure. He'll pay a pretty price to get you back, I'll wager."

Rory nearly laughed at the absurd notion. The baron wouldn't pay anything. The old goat probably wouldn't piss on him if he were on fire. Saying as much, however, wasn't going to help. No one, other than Maxwell, would believe him. He was going to be taken hostage, no matter what he said. *Then I'll die in this horrid forest for certain.* Fearful and unable to explain the futility of his abduction, he lashed out as he'd learned to do when frightened and cornered. "You can't have me, you brute!" He kicked at the man's crotch and clawed at his face, even knowing it could lead to his quick death.

Instead of stopping him with the point of his knife, the brigand merely avoided his assault, captured his arms in a strong grip, spun him around and wrestled him into a tight hug. The despicable robber had the temerity to laugh as he did so. Rory thrashed and pounded at the man's arms, but to no avail. It didn't take long for him to become exhausted at the effort, and in the end, he lay limp and panting in his grasp.

"If you are done trying to escape the inevitable, we shall take our leave now." The words were said not unkindly.

Resigned temporarily to his fate, Rory didn't struggle as the brigand hauled him away from the carriage. Another man, surprisingly dressed as a monk, approached. "Evan, let me tend to the boy. He's little more than a child."

"I am *not* a child." He'd always had trouble guarding his tongue, but this was a sore topic for him. He knew his short stature and lack of facial hair made him look young and helpless. Those assumptions by others made him vulnerable. To prove his point, he started to struggle again.

The man called 'Evan' tightened his grip. "Thank you but no. This is my burden to bear—and it's not as bad as it looks." The man's laughing tone was clear.

Rory tried to kick backward, pressing himself against the man's body. That's when he felt a frightening hardness. A shiver streaked down his spine, and he went limp again. This was a danger he hadn't contemplated. Now that it was obvious, he didn't want to do anything to encourage the man's interest.

"Wise boy." The words were nearly a whisper against his ear.

The sound of them, coupled with the tickling warm breath against his skin, made Rory shiver again. His breathing came in quick pants that he labored to get under control. *Show no fear.* That was a lesson hard learned, and it would serve him well in this situation.

"You, valet, take my words back to the baron. He's to have a half-year's-worth of taxes to be delivered to this spot in a fortnight if he wishes to see his son again."

Maxwell drew himself up straight and looked down at the brigand as only the man could, despite his shorter stature. "I will do no such thing. The coachman will take back the message. I go where my young master does."

That caused the ruffians around them to laugh. "The boy won't have need of your pampering service," the leader said. "We live rough in the forest. The experience might do him some good, actually."

Rory didn't know what to say or what to do. He'd never been without Maxwell, and as hard as he could be with the devoted servant, the thought of being without his company was terrifying. Only pride kept him from sending the man a pleading look or speaking up to keep him.

It didn't matter, in any event. Maxwell wasn't to be deterred. "Take me with you, or I'll shall find a way to follow." His gaze slanted sideways toward the archers still pointing arrows at them. "Regardless of the potential consequences."

"Will the baron pay more for us to release you, as well?"

"No." Maxwell's expression and tone never changed from his determined haughtiness. The man had courage. There was no denying that.

Rory knew a measure of gratitude and tried to show it in his eyes before saying, "He means it. The stubborn old man has always been a thorn in my side, but he does have his uses."

There was silence while everyone waited for the leader of the brigands to decide. His chest rose and fell against Rory's back on a big sigh. "Very well. It might make my job easier, I suppose." He stepped away from the carriage, dragging Rory with him. "Turn around and go back to the baron with my demands," he shouted to the coachman and footman.

They were two of the laziest servants in the baron's household, but they would high-tail it back to the safety of the castle, that was for certain. Their message would fall on deaf ears, however. Rory knew that for sure and so did Maxwell, no doubt. Perhaps the man wanted to join the brigands rather than continue to serve the baron or Rory. No one could blame him if that were the case.

They waited until the carriage was back on its way before the brigands lowered their weapons and celebrated their success with muted grins and back-slapping. A large, homely man tossed the coin purse in his large hand. "A decent haul, Evan, even without the ransom."

"Good. We shall wait for the baron to send us more. Come, young sir. I will show you to your temporary home." He loosened his grip enough for Rory to walk by his side, although he still held him close.

As he stepped off the road and into the dark shadows of the forest, Rory hid his fear with bravado. "You will rue this decision to kidnap me."

The brigand squeezed Rory's waist. "Oh, I doubt it. I'm already enjoying my time with you."

Rory managed to jab his elbow into the oaf's stomach. "You will keep your hands to yourself."

The brigand merely chuckled, even as he rubbed the spot where the elbow had landed. "I do love a challenge, but worry not, young sir. No one will harm you here. You have my word on it."

"As if that means anything."

The man didn't respond right away. "It has to. I have little else left to give." And on that odd declaration, they continued making their way deeper into the woods in silence.

About the Author

Samantha Cayto is a Boston-area native who practices as a business lawyer by day while writing erotic romance at night—the steamier the better. She likes to push the envelope when it comes to writing about passion and is delighted other women agree that guy-on-guy sex is the hottest ever.

She lives a typical suburban life with her husband, three kids and four dogs. Her children don't understand why they can't read what she writes, but her husband is always willing to lend her a hand—and anything else—when she needs to choreograph a scene.

Samantha loves to hear from readers. You can find her contact information, website details and author profile page at https://www.pride-publishing.com

Sign up for our newsletter and find out about all our romance book releases, eBook sales and promotions, sneak peeks and FREE romance books!

www.ingramcontent.com/pod-product-compliance
Lightning Source LLC
LaVergne TN
LVHW090942080826
845145LV00003B/856

* 9 7 8 1 8 0 2 5 0 5 3 0 6 *